T0328505

THE GIRL WHO CHASED OTTERS

THE GIRL WHO CHASED OTTERS

A story about friendship and falling in love

SALLY PARTRIDGE

Publication © Modjaji Books 2021
Text © Sally Partridge 2021
First published in 2021 by Modjaji Books Pty Ltd
www.modjajibooks.co.za

ISBN 978-1-928433-28-6 (Print)
ISBN 978-1-928433-29-3 (ePub)

Edited by Tracey Hawthorne
Cover design by Carla Kreuser
Typesetting by Monique Cleghorn

Set in Legacy Serif

To all the survivors.
Life is hard, but the bumps are temporary. Keep moving and you'll get to where you need to be in the end.

1

Nathan watched Olivia from the back of the class, in his usual spot near the windows. He liked it at the back, where he was less distracted by people talking around him. Usually the slackers took residence of these prime seats, but Nathan's position was never challenged, as though his invisibility covered the entire desk. He'd been this way since he started school and would probably continue till matric.

He didn't mind. He liked being invisible. It made life uncomplicated and meant his days passed quickly and without incident.

Olivia sat hunched in her seat, shoulders slouched, staring morosely at a cluster of girls bent over a magazine they'd hidden inside a textbook.

Nathan watched her slow sigh, the long intake of breath, the slight rise of her shoulders, followed by the deflation. Her body relaxed back into a slump.

Something was different. Typically, her straight back would be bent over her work, and she'd be writing at a furious pace, trying to keep up with Miss De Waal's notes from the front of the class. They were the only ones in class who really cared about schoolwork. It was a connection of sorts, like being part of a secret contest where the winner was the one who scored highest in tests. Well, not so much English. His marks were average at best.

She'd also tried something different with her hair. Her long braid had been replaced by a low, untidy bun, a knock-off version of the ones worn by the popular girls. Since the day they'd started talking to each other in grade 8 she'd always, always worn the same braid.

Nathan scrunched up his face in concentration, his lips moving as he sought an explanation for her peculiar behaviour.

She wants to be like them.

He realised he'd been holding his breath. He didn't like sudden change, and on top of it, he hadn't heard a single word Miss De Waal had said.

Nathan craned his head slightly and moved his lips again, an irritating habit he couldn't shake. When his brain processed information, he had little control over the rest of his body. He shook his head vigorously, earning a momentary glance or two. His classmates were used to his stims and didn't even bother teasing him about them now. He was simply that-weird-kid-Nathan.

This judgement had once infuriated him, but he didn't care any more. He kept to himself, being as polite as possible to those he encountered, which worked well as a strategy. It was easier not to engage others in conversation. If he did, he'd inadvertently say the wrong thing, info dump or upset someone, and that was usually when the wheels started coming off. So, now, he wasn't bullied or teased or even pitied. He was largely ignored, which suited him fine.

But Olivia intrigued him. After all, she was the closest thing to a friend he had at Conradie High School.

He sat up a little straighter and thought about it. If she wanted to be popular, then she was going about it the wrong way. Simply changing her hairstyle wasn't going to work. There was a strategy to it, a checklist.

His teeth worried at his lower lip and his feet started bouncing up and down. Should he tell her? His father had drilled into him that poking his nose into other people's business was wrong. He'd accepted this little revelation with much frustration. 'But they're doing it wrong,' he'd whined to his dad. 'If I could just—'

'No. Leave them alone. It's not your business.'

'But Dad—'

'It's how the world works, Nathan. People need to work out their own mistakes. It's not for you to tell them. Especially not your mother. It drives her mad.'

He tried to focus his attention on the lesson, but Olivia was being far too fascinating.

She was doodling in the margin of her notebook with a pencil and shielding the drawing with her other hand, afraid of anyone seeing it. She was oblivious that this would only draw more attention. Craning his neck, Nathan managed to spot the picture. It was an animal of some kind. An otter, maybe.

Olivia was an animal lover. She often smiled when a bird appeared at the classroom window, and her pink Typo notebook was covered in turtles.

As he watched, a couple of girls shifted their gaze to Olivia's small hands and began to mutter among themselves.

'Olivia, is that something you wish to share with the rest of the class?'

Olivia jerked upright, wisps of her dark hair escaping the bun, and glanced around wildly to see if anyone was looking at her. 'No, Miss,' she said in a panicked voice.

One of the girls at the front of class, Mandy, a particularly aggressive girl, gave a derisive snort. Olivia blushed scarlet, and in seconds she was completely flustered. She turned the page in her notebook and held her pencil at the ready, her fingers trembling slightly.

Nathan shifted in his seat and waited for the muttering around him to recede. His mind felt like it was full of bees. Counting sometimes helped. *One hundred. Ninety-nine. Ninety-eight.*

When the bell rang for the start of break, he grabbed his bag and dashed out as fast as he could, desperate for the stillness promised by the outside world.

Sitting under his normal tree, he tried to quieten his mind by watching a flock of pigeons weave through the grey and cloudy sky, but even this created its own noise in his head. When the flock turned, seemingly in unison, he could see the transition as a diagram, a thermodynamic system of individual birds becoming components of the whole, unfolding one by one, in reaction to the one before.

Nathan was so absorbed by the wheeling pigeons that he didn't notice the shadow approaching across the grass, and only realised he had company when he looked down to see a pair of size-five leather lace-up shoes in front of him.

'I've been looking everywhere for you,' Olivia said, clutching her lunchbox the same way she held her books – close to her chest, protectively.

He blinked up at her. She was standing directly underneath a patch of sun breaking through the clouds, her face obscured by shadow. Behind her, the giant billboard advertising whitening toothpaste flashed a massive pearly smile.

'Can you move a bit to the left? I can't see your face.'

She did as instructed, and he relaxed.

'Your hair looks nice today.'

Nathan risked a quick glance at her face to test her response. Her expression was close to the one his mom had worn the previous afternoon when he'd tried to explain his mathematics homework to her. Disbelief, maybe? Although disbelief didn't quite fit. Confusion? Surprise? Yes, surprise made more sense.

Olivia pushed a strand of hair behind her ear. 'Do you really think so?'

The question took him aback. 'Yes. I said so, didn't I?'

She blinked in confusion, and he decided a change of subject was needed.

'Why are you looking for me?'

She hesitated. 'You rushed out of class today and I wanted to check if you were okay.'

'I'm fine. My head was a little full this morning, that's all.'

She nodded like this made perfect sense, but still made no move to leave. Her eyes kept travelling to where the other girls in her grade sat in a large circle, and Nathan remembered that she had no group of her own, but rather moved from cluster to cluster, never staying long enough for anyone to notice her absence when she left.

'Why are you all the way over here, away from everyone else?' she asked.

'I don't need company to eat a sandwich,' he said, adding, 'and I don't mind sitting by myself.'

She wrinkled her forehead. 'But don't you get lonely?'

'No. I have a friend. He just goes to a different school.'

'That's not what I meant,' she said, rolling her eyes. 'I mean friends here, in this school.'

Nathan shrugged. 'I don't need any more friends. And I have you to talk to if I really wanted to.'

She didn't react to his statement, but her bright brown eyes scanned the field, lingering on the girls from class – Mandy, Jill, Blaize and Virginie.

'If you want to sit with them so badly, why don't you?'

She jumped and clutched her lunchbox even more tightly. 'How do you know I want to sit with them? Did someone say something?'

He lowered his eyes and laughed to himself so that she didn't think he was laughing at her. 'It's obvious by the way you look at them all the time.'

She sucked in her bottom lip. 'Do I? Have you seen me staring?'

He nodded. 'Among other things.'

Without waiting for an invitation, she sat down on the grass opposite him and crossed her legs. A graze on her elbow had been dabbed with iodine and it made a criss-cross pattern on her dark skin, like the skull and crossbones on a pirate flag.

'What else do I do?' she asked.

Nathan tore his eyes from her elbow and settled his gaze on a blade of grass near her right foot. It was easy to talk to Olivia. 'You changed your hair, you don't concentrate in class any more, and your skirt is shorter.'

He pulled up a clump of grass and started arranging the blades into a neat line. She was going to accuse him of stalking her or call him a weirdo or storm off or something. He waited for her angry response, but she didn't move. He risked a quick look at her face. She wasn't upset at all. He watched her closely, and when she lowered her gaze to meet his, he quickly looked back at his little assembly line.

'Can you see inside everyone like that?'

He moved the blades around in order of size. 'I can't see inside people.'

'But you understand how they work.'

He considered her words. 'It's just tribal behaviour. It's not like I'm picking up anything that's not there for everyone to see.'

She smiled. 'Not everyone can see it, though. I think you're probably the only one, except for the teachers, maybe. Or Sherlock Holmes.'

'Sherlock Holmes isn't a real person. He's a character invented by Arthur Conan Doyle, which you know, because we read one of the novels last year.'

'You know what I mean. You have a unique insight into the world.'

He shrugged. His father often referred to him as 'his little Sherlock Holmes', as if he was some sort of genius who could solve crimes. He wasn't. He was just particularly observant and took an interest in things other people didn't. Unfortunately, this was a characteristic that alienated him from people.

Olivia opened her lunchbox, picked up half a sandwich and took a large bite. It was Marmite and cheese. 'So, explain this tribal behaviour to me that you know so much about,' she said through a mouthful. She pointed to two grade 11 boys kicking a soccer ball to each other. 'What's so tribal about what they're doing?'

This one was so obvious he could've laughed. He was surprised she didn't see it. 'You see how hard they're kicking the ball? Aggression is one of the traits that's linked to social status. Fearlessness is another one. They're acting pretty typically for alpha males, actually.'

She lowered the sandwich, which had been halfway to her mouth. 'What other traits are there?'

'Playfulness. Sociability. But there are other factors too. Have you ever heard of something called homophily?'

She shook her head.

'Okay. Um ... it means that people enjoy the company of those most like themselves. Dissimilarity leads to dislike, which is why there are so many different fragmented groups in school. All the people with the same characteristics cluster together.'

'You sound like you memorised the textbook or something,' she said, mid-chew. She touched her hair absently and added, 'Do people know that they're doing all those things?'

'Probably not consciously, even though it's pretty obvious.'

A moment of contemplation passed between them. It was bewildering to him that she didn't see what he saw. He wasn't doing anything special, just paying attention.

'How do you know so much?'

He shrugged again. 'I just know.' What he really wanted to say was, *It's basic natural science.*

'Could you teach me what you know, about the traits and everything?'

He couldn't see any sign that she was making fun of him. There was no twist to the mouth, no suppressed smile. She was simply staring at him, her eyes expectant.

'I suppose so. It's not rocket science or anything.'

She grinned, which made him grin a little bit too. Her smile was infectious like that. She finished her sandwich in silence.

Nathan decided that he didn't mind her company. He watched her study the progress of a butterfly with almost child-like glee. He liked that she got so much enjoyment out of such a simple thing. He followed the insect's jittery flight, its fragile wings looking almost translucent in the dim patches of sunlight peeking through the clouds.

He hoped Olivia would choose to sit with him again, even after she realised that all she had to do was open her eyes and look.

2

Nathan enjoyed music, the more complicated the better. Genre didn't bother him as much as it did other people. It always amused him how much importance his classmates placed on music taste. Anything to fit in. At the moment the in-thing was international dance music, which didn't sound like music at all, but rather a series of beats and samples hashed together to create a pleasing sound.

Nathan loved instrumental pieces, both old and new. His Spotify playlist featured complicated Mozart symphonies alongside How to Destroy Angels and Nine Inch Nails.

He lay on the grass with his earbuds in and watched the distant confusion of clouds swirling above him while his thoughts remained firmly fixed on Olivia. He was happy to help her, although a small voice at the back of his mind reminded him that helping her might see her change from the current Olivia into someone else. Still, he wanted to make her happy. He liked it when she was happy.

His musings were interrupted by the arrival of the family's

labrador, Wendy. She bounded up to him through the open sliding door and shoved a wet nose into his stomach.

He sat upright to scratch her head, as his best friend Mohendra stepped on to the patio with his laptop tucked under his arm. As usual, his friend had used too much hair gel and his hair stood up in sharp, unnatural points. Nathan had been wanting to tell him for ages that it probably didn't have the desired effect on girls that Mohendra wanted.

Nathan pulled out his earphones and brushed the grass out of his hair. 'You're just in time for supper again,' he said. 'It's like you plan it that way.'

Mohendra grinned. 'Maybe I'm just really good at timing.'

Mohendra used to be a neighbour. He and Nathan had grown up together, and when Mohendra's family moved a few suburbs away, Mohendra had continued to visit as often as he had before – even though he'd moved to another school, his father's alma mater in Wynberg. They'd been best friends since childhood.

The two boys went inside, where Nathan's mother was already setting out plates on the black-marble table. The boys perched on the wooden bar stools Nathan's grandfather had carved himself, and waited expectantly for the arrival of the beef stir-fry steaming itself to a soggy death on the stove.

Mohendra placed his laptop on the counter. 'What do you feel like playing later? You up for some PUBG?'

'Sure. Your streaming headphones are still here anyway,' replied Nathan, thinking of his friend's neon-green headset that was his signature Twitch gimmick.

Mohendra opened his laptop and called up the command-prompt box. He had a new desktop wallpaper depicting a cosplayer dressed as Misty from Pokémon, who was wearing little more than a thin length of yellow material across her chest.

Mohendra had a problem with girls. Nathan knew from experience that there was a folder full of pictures on the desktop, and, worse, a folder of explicit content hidden on the hard drive somewhere. As far as Nathan knew, Mohendra had never had a girlfriend, but he spoke about hardly anything else.

Nathan enjoyed the simplicity of Mohendra's friendship. He was never jealous or manipulative, and he was extremely mindful of Nathan's stims. It was easy to talk to Mohendra about games and hardware, and even girls, even though Mohendra did most of the talking when that particular topic was raised.

Nathan never spoke about being on the spectrum and the challenges that came with it. Once, at Mohendra's house, he'd heard Mrs Chetty on the phone encouraging her niece not to vaccinate her new baby. It had been hard to hear. Nathan knew anti-vaxxers believed vaccines caused autism and thought that causing a massive worldwide measles epidemic was preferable to having a kid like him. He made a point to never bring up the subject.

After a hastily swallowed meal, they pushed their plates away, retrieved their laptops, and got straight into the game. Nathan had adjusted his game settings so that he used the keyboard rather than the mouse, which he found slow and constricting. His fingers moved quickly across the keys, his eyes even faster.

First-person-shooter games were his favourite. Although he found them tricky at first, he would soon crack the formula behind the game code and could anticipate where the enemy would most likely appear, and the time when the health drops would occur. His kill count continued to rise rapidly as the game progressed, while Mohendra's trailed.

They were a few hours into the game when Nathan noticed a hand waving above his monitor. He hit pause and looked up.

'I've been trying to get your attention for five minutes,' said Mohendra.

'I didn't hear you.'

'Clearly.'

Nathan waited patiently for his friend to say whatever he wanted to say. It was better when Mohendra was playing online at home, and they could chat through Discord. It was hard to concentrate with Mohendra right there, especially when he was clearly worked up over a girl again.

'It's Karen,' he sighed.

Nathan nodded. Of course it was. She was friends with Mohendra's sister, Verashni. The way he'd described her had made her sound like a famous model with the longest legs in the world and freckles that were close to being indecent.

'She's sleeping over this weekend.'

'So?'

'So how am I supposed to sleep with her right there in the other room?'

'The same way you sleep every other night.'

Outside the window, the light was rapidly transforming to dark, and an army of cirrocumulus clouds was beginning to march across the sky. Nathan, realising he was becoming distracted again, forced himself to concentrate on what Mohendra was saying.

'You should see the way she flutters her eyelashes at me. I think she's teasing me. She does it on purpose.'

'Probably. She wants you to notice her.'

Mohendra snapped his fingers. 'You see! I knew she was doing it on purpose.'

Nathan nodded and looked longingly at his stalled game. He'd been really into it, but there was no way they'd be able to carry on with Mohendra worked up as he was. They'd have to continue playing some other time.

'You think I should ask my sister if it's true? Would she even tell me the truth if it was?'

'Why would she lie?'

Mohendra shook his head slowly. 'Girls lie all the time.'

Nathan made a mental note to check that fact. He couldn't imagine Olivia lying to anyone. He leaned across to his laptop and pressed escape to bring up his Spotify playlist. He scrolled down to the next band name that began with D. He liked to control the music when they gamed at his house.

When they were at Mohendra's house, Mohendra set his playlist to random, and the songs always jarred with each other, making it impossible for Nathan to concentrate. Nathan suspected that could've been Mohendra's strategy all along. His best friend knew he liked everything to be in its correct order. But to be fair, it was probably the only strategy he could employ to win against Nathan in a game.

'Would I even date a ginger?' Mohendra wondered.

'What does her hair colour have to do with it?'

'It's not just her hair colour. She's a ginger. Like I'm Indian and you're white.'

'Ginger isn't an actual race group.'

Nathan was starting to become frustrated with the conversation, and it was making him grumpy. 'Maybe you should decide whether you actually like Karen before asking your sister if the feeling is reciprocated.'

Mohendra threw his hands up in the air. 'Fine! You're right. You're always right. Do you want to finish the game or not?'

Nathan instantly relaxed, relieved that the topic was closed.

They played for another two hours before Nathan's mother chased Mohendra home. When he was gone, she stood in the kitchen doorway while Nathan rolled up his cables. He looked up and guessed that she wanted to talk or else she would be watching *MasterChef* like she did every other night.

'Is it true that all girls lie?' he asked her.

She narrowed her eyes. 'Did Mohendra tell you that?'

'Ja.'

'It's a generalisation. Everyone lies. Girls don't lie any more than boys do.' She sounded amused.

3

Olivia was back during lunch break the next day. The tips of her shoes gleaming with moisture from the wet grass announced her arrival.

Nathan looked up and she looked down, her books clutched tightly to her chest and her bag bulging with more. His stomach dipped. She was bouncing lightly on the balls of her feet and loose strands of her hair floated lazily in the breeze. Her hair seemed to exist in its own universe with its own set of rules.

'Hello.'

'Hi.'

'I'm back.'

'I see that.'

She rewarded him with a rare open-mouthed smile, revealing just for a moment all her neat white teeth. 'You're so funny, Nathan. You should be a comedian or something.' She sat down on the moist grass opposite him, folding her jersey underneath her legs so that she didn't get her skirt wet.

'I never tell jokes at school.'

'But you're so funny!'

Was she teasing him? He couldn't tell.

When he didn't respond, she cleared her throat. 'So, I was thinking about what you said yesterday and I think you may be on to something.'

'On to what?'

'The secret to being popular.'

'You mean observation and logic?'

She tossed back her head and laughed, making even more hair escape round her face.

Settling back against the tree, he said, 'So, you want me to help you become popular? I can only tell you what I know about social behaviour, nothing else.'

She leaned forward, her eyes widening. 'But that's exactly what I want. You'll help me, won't you? I'm terrible at talking to people.'

He looked at his knees and began worrying at a loose stitch in his grey sock. 'So am I.'

'But that's because you're you. I need help with me.'

'There's nothing wrong with you.'

She smiled the sad smile he didn't like, the one that wasn't really a smile, but rather a frown trying to hide.

He sighed. 'What do you want to know?'

'Everything!'

'That's too broad.'

'How to speak to people, then.'

'You're speaking to me right now.'

She thumped the ground with her fists, making him jump a little. 'You know what I mean! Stop being so literal.'

'This is how I talk.'

He knew their conversation would reach a dead end eventually. It happened every time someone tried to speak to him, even his best friend. At those moments Nathan preferred to just keep quiet. It was simpler that way. But this time he didn't want the conversation to stop. There was an urgency inside him to hear more of her voice. It made no sense. 'Tell me about the otter,' he said.

She blinked in surprise. 'The what?'

'The otter from your book.'

She gaped at him. As clarity dawned, her eyes flashed open wide. 'Were you spying on me, Nathan Langdon? Is that why you know so much about me?'

Nathan jerked back in alarm, dropping his lunchbox on the grass. He quickly retrieved it before his sandwiches got dirty. 'I could see what you were drawing from my desk,' he said, without looking up.

He waited, wondering if she really did think he was spying on her. He felt a blush coming on, the heat growing in his face. He hated that he couldn't control what his body did.

To his surprise, she started laughing.

'Otters are my favourite animal. I'm a little bit obsessed with them.'

'Why?'

'You really want to know?'

'Yes. I wouldn't have asked you if I didn't.'

'Okay, okay. No need to get irritated with me. I think they're cute.' She began playing with the frayed strap of her bag. 'I would keep one as a pet if I could.'

They fell back into silence, only this time, she was smiling.

'I wasn't spying on you and I wasn't getting irritated,' he said.

'If you say so.'

She was being purposely difficult. He frowned as he replayed their conversation in his mind. 'I wasn't trying to be rude on purpose,' he clarified.

She smiled. 'Don't worry about it.'

She leaned forward and brushed some drops of dew from his knee. He kept still till she was done, not even breathing. He knew she knew he didn't like being touched. It must be a test of some kind.

Somewhere far away the bell rang. He didn't want to get up, didn't want this moment to end.

Oblivious to his state of mind, Olivia stood up quickly and picked up her bag with both hands. 'I'll be back,' she said, with an indecipherable smile.

Nathan decided that if it had been a test of some kind, he'd passed.

The next morning, the thick blanket of grey cloud had stretched out across the entire sky. The promised sunshine was delayed for another day.

Nathan's mother had left a school scarf on his bed, a slash of black against the green covers. He wound it around his neck, then pulled the strap of his backpack over his shoulder. He knew she didn't trust him to dress warmly on cold days, which was why she'd come into his room while he was in the bathroom and got his thick socks and scarf out his chest of drawers and put them where he could see them. He wasn't grateful or irritated. He just accepted that his mother needed to do it because it made her feel like she was helping him without him knowing that she was.

He passed her on his way to the front door. She was standing in the kitchen, placing his father's morning newspapers in a neat pile. 'Do you have your lunch?' she asked.

'Yes, thank you.'

It was a ridiculous question. His mother always packed his lunch into his bag for him, every single day since he'd started school. Whether or not she trusted him to make his own lunch was still up for debate. He'd long ago stopped trying to understand his mother.

Olivia was waiting for him outside the school gate. A happiness grenade exploded inside him, but he kept his features impassive. She'd reverted to the messy plait that hung down her back, although her skirt was still way above the regulation two fingers above the knee line.

'Hi, Nathan,' she said, smiling.

'Hi, Olivia.'

She fell into step beside him. 'So, what's my next lesson going to be about? Can you teach me how to start thinking like you?'

He shook his head in confusion. 'Why would you want to think like me?'

She didn't answer at first. 'I just want to be normal. If I thought like you, then I'd know what I needed to do to be like everyone else.'

Nathan's forehead creased into a frown. To him, Olivia was perfect. 'But you are normal,' he said.

She smiled, and the alarm he felt subsided slightly. 'That's very sweet of you to say, Nathan, but I don't feel normal. I feel like an outcast, like there's something wrong with me. And you did promise me a lesson.'

Nathan opened his mouth to correct her, but quickly closed it again. He hadn't promised her anything. He'd just agreed to help her. It wasn't the same thing, and he was sure she knew that. He wondered briefly if she was employing some form of guile to get her own way. Mohendra believed guile was just one of the many tools girls used to manipulate guys, and had warned Nathan on numerous occasions to be careful when dealing with them. Was Olivia being manipulative? He didn't want to believe that she was. The thought raced around his head, gaining momentum until the speed of it forced the words out his mouth. 'I didn't promise you anything.'

She blushed. 'What?'

'I didn't promise that I'd help you. I said I would. I didn't promise.'

'Okay, okay,' she said, reaching for his arm. Her hand hovered in mid-air awkwardly for a minute before falling limply back at her side. 'I forget sometimes that you think differently to other people.'

He nodded. That was true.

'But you're still going to help me, right?' she asked.

'Yes. I said I would. Why would I suddenly change my mind?'

Her face creased up. 'Never mind, Nathan. Don't worry about it.' She made a move to walk away. 'I'll see you at lunchtime, okay?'

'Okay.'

Nathan watched her go, suddenly panicking about whether he'd screwed up something between them. A guy coming towards him crashed into his shoulder, and he quickly moved aside so as not to stand in the way of traffic. He didn't like feeling so flustered so early in the day.

He ducked into the boys' bathroom and went to the last basin at the end of the row, the one where the enamel was least chipped. He gripped the sides of the basin and bent his head, causing his untidy blond hair to fall in his face. Inexplicably, she'd managed to unnerve him again and it was taking longer to pull himself back together. He needed to calm down.

One hundred. Ninety-nine. Ninety-eight. Ninety-seven.

He was breathing too fast. When he was worked up like this, his brain started doing strange things, like counting everything he could. The tiles on the floor stood out, begging him to count them. He forced himself to look away.

Pulling the cuff of his school jersey over his fingers, he opened the tap to wash his face. When he looked up again, he noticed that he'd forgotten to brush his hair that morning. Again. Attempting to flatten it was a futile exercise. The hair at the back was tangled from sleeping on it all night. Not that anyone would notice. He'd once walked around all day with odd socks on and not one person had said anything.

Still, he wondered if Olivia had seen. He noted everything about her, like the fact that she was wearing a blue hairband instead of the usual black one, that she'd scuffed the side of her shoe since yesterday, that she'd forgotten her English textbook at home. He smiled at his reflection. Maybe she had noticed. After all, she was the only person in school who really saw him. Not only that, she wanted to see him. She wanted to spend break with him. The thought made all the air rush out of his lungs.

He would do anything he could to keep her coming back, even humouring this silly idea of hers, of teaching her to think like him.

4

'Do you know who Charles Darwin is?'

Olivia looked at him lopsidedly. Her head was balanced on her hand, which in turn was balanced on her knee. Her limp plait hung across her shoulder.

'What kind of question is that? Of course I do.'

Nathan straightened up. 'Okay, so you know all about natural selection?'

Her expression was unreadable.

'He discovered that animals that looked and behaved in a certain way to fit in with their environment were the ones most likely to survive.'

The unreadable expression remained.

'You see,' he said, 'it's all about fitting in with the rest of the group.'

She looked dubious. 'Are you comparing me to a finch right now?'

'No. I'm trying to give you a basic idea of the principle.'

It felt good to help her, but he would never admit that out loud.

She rummaged in her bag for a notebook and placed her denim stationery bag on the ground. She unzipped it and took out a pen. 'I want to write down what you're saying,' she said, pulling off the top of the pen with her teeth. 'Even if you secretly compare me to a bird.'

He stared at his shoes to avoid her gaze. The sole of the left one was scuffed along the edges and there was a hole growing underneath. Even the laces were starting to fray. He would have to tell his mother that he needed new shoes, even though he didn't want to. She would accuse him of not looking after his things, even though he'd worn the shoes for more than a year and the damage was due to normal wear and tear. He would get less difficulty from his father.

'Nathan? Did you hear what I just said?'

He returned his attention to Olivia. He liked the way her eyes glittered in the sun, like there were tiny gold flakes floating in the irises. 'I got distracted, sorry.'

'I've noticed that about you. You go blank sometimes. Does your mind travel somewhere else when that happens?'

'It's hard for me to focus on too many things at the same time. I get stuck on one thing. It's ... it's something I live with. You get used to it.' He spoke quickly and breathlessly, wanting to get the explanation over and done with. He hated explaining the way his brain worked. It changed the way people looked at him and that was one thing he could do without.

She nodded, although he doubted that she could relate to what he was saying. People seldom did. 'I asked you how a person could adapt themselves to be more like other people, to fit in?'

He began winding one of his shoelaces between his fingers. 'First, you have to identify the alpha female in the group you want to fit in with. Who's the one everybody tries to be like the most?'

She thought for a moment and looked over her shoulder at the group of girls sitting on the grass in a wide circle. Their laughter was clearly audible. She swallowed nervously. 'Virginie. She's the alpha.'

He followed her gaze. Virginie was surrounded by girls from their grade. Nathan knew all about the skinny blonde girl with the sky-blue eyes. She was very rich. Her parents owned a wine farm in Franschhoek. She'd never spoken to him, but she'd laughed at him often. He didn't think she was a very nice girl, but he didn't want to say anything to Olivia in case she felt differently. Besides, he was assuming, and assumptions were often false. 'Is that why your skirt is so short? Because she wears hers like that?'

Olivia blushed as brightly as a strawberry. 'Ja. Isn't that what you're supposed to do? Copy them? That's what you said I had to do.'

'That's only a small part of it.'

She tilted her head and peered at him sideways. 'What else must I do?' The question came out quickly, desperately.

It made him uncomfortable that she felt so strongly about changing herself. He shifted position and she mirrored his actions, crossing her legs.

He sighed. 'Total assimilation is going to take a lot of work. Are you sure you really want to change yourself?'

She wrote the words 'total assimilation' in her notebook, her lips moving as she spelled them out to herself. 'What else?' she asked eagerly. She was stubbornly ignoring his question.

He hated when people did that, but as much as it was a trait he despised, he didn't mind overlooking it in Olivia. 'Okay. The first thing you need to work on is how you speak to them. You're too nervous and your voice goes higher when you speak to any of the girls in class. Try to match their tone exactly. No lower, no higher. And don't say "um" when you speak to them.'

Her eyebrows knitted together into a frown. 'Are you serious?'

'Yes.'

'I didn't know my voice did that.' She hugged her notebook, not realising that her voice had just risen an octave higher.

'You also need to watch your expressions. Don't look so sad all the time.'

She looked at him in surprise. 'Do I really look sad all the time?'

'You look sad right now.'

She dropped her gaze to the ground. 'Oh.'

Nathan was in his element, unable to stop himself. 'Can you act neutral, like nothing's bothering you? When they talk to you, try to be friendly and don't get flustered.'

She wrote: 'Act more confident.' 'Anything else?' she asked, twirling her pen between her fingers.

He was really doing this, teaching her how to be popular. Usually he enjoyed explaining things to people, but he wasn't enjoying teaching this particular subject to Olivia. He didn't think she needed to change. It felt wrong, but he didn't want to stop. 'You have to attend essential group gatherings.' He said the words reluctantly.

'What the hell are those?'

'Parties.'

'Oh. There's a big party this weekend in the community hall. Do you think I should go to that?'

'Definitely.' *Definitely not*, is what he'd really wanted to say.

She didn't seem excited by the idea, but he couldn't be sure. She was already adopting a neutral expression, making her face impossible to read, but that might have been his imagination.

'You make it sound so easy,' she said. 'It's amazing no one's thought of it before.'

'Well, they have.'

She laughed and rolled her eyes. 'No, man. Normal people, I mean.'

He sighed and looked up at the sky, suddenly mesmerised by a passing plane. A Boeing 747, he noted.

'I'm going to try some of your tips today. Let's see how far I get.'

She spent the remainder of break practising looking neutral in the selfie view of her phone camera. It involved a lot of pouting.

They didn't speak again.

Nathan wasn't going to be seeing Olivia till later in the afternoon, but it was difficult keeping his thoughts focused on anything else. In geography, while the rest of the class were bent over diagrams of South African river systems, Nathan sat back in his chair, wondering about Olivia's progress and the different scenarios that could play out as a result of her actions.

He was acutely aware of Virginie behind him. Even though they were supposed to be working, her friends chatted to her non-stop. She liked the attention. If Olivia didn't threaten Virginie's throne as alpha female, then she should be fine. She would just be another acolyte.

'Is everything okay, Nathan? Do you need help with your drawing?'

Nathan looked up into the well-meaning but slightly cautious face of Mr Wright, a youngish man with a light-brown beard and spectacles. 'No, I've already done them,' he said, retrieving his completed diagrams from the back of his notebook.

'Oh, I see ... Well, maybe you can read quietly while the rest of the class catches up.' With a quick smile that made his moustache twitch, Mr Wright continued up the aisle to check on the other students.

Nathan took a book about robotics out of his bag, confident that no one would even look twice at what he was reading, least of all Mr Wright, who was one of those frustrating adults who didn't feel entirely comfortable talking to him, like he was some strange hybrid made up of half unpredictable child and half know-it-all. It just proved, thought Nathan, as he opened the book to where he'd last left off, that adults were as prone to group thinking as teenagers were. He understood why his classmates treated him differently – after all, they were still learning social skills – but Mr Wright should know better. The fear of the 'other' that he displayed was a characteristic of ignorance. And the only thing that made Nathan an 'other', was that his brain worked a little differently.

Teachers shouldn't be ignorant, yet it was one characteristic most of them shared. In fact, it was a characteristic most adults in general shared. Yet most people, like Olivia, were unable to see this. It was like a blindness that only he, Nathan, was immune to.

Still, it wasn't his place to point this out to anyone, because then he'd be the annoying know-it-all again.

He turned the page and began the next chapter, 'Electronics and Circuitry: An Advanced Guide'.

5

As it turned out, Olivia was a quick learner. By the last period she'd already earned smiles from two of the girls in Virginie's circle, Jill and Blaize, by politely passing a note from one to the other. She hadn't been too eager or indifferent, but had simply smiled warmly when the note had come her way. Both Jill and Blaize had responded well to her attempt at friendliness. It was only Mandy who remained dubious.

Olivia had done brilliantly, Nathan thought. If she carried on like this, she'd quickly gain the acceptance of the other girls. He noticed that she walked to the next class with her back straight and her expression relaxed. A grade 12 boy jumped out of her way as she walked past, and her demeanour almost slipped when a blush flared on her cheeks, but she covered it up well by smiling sweetly at the girl next to her, like she'd found the whole encounter funny.

Nathan watched her progress with interest. She was determined to follow his advice to the letter, going as far as matching the tone of teachers who asked her questions in class, even though he hadn't told her to do that. It didn't surprise him. Olivia was an excellent student who got consistently good marks. In fact, she was always the forerunner for the top-student accolade.

He wanted to ask her about it, but she hadn't come to talk to him again. As comfortable as he was around her, he still found it difficult initiating conversation. He'd tried a hundred times in his head, but every time he passed her in the hallways he found himself walking straight past. Sometimes she smiled at him, but he didn't think that counted as an invitation.

By the end of the week, Olivia had started chatting to some of the other girls between classes. She was only slightly jumpy, and Nathan made a mental note to tell her to stop peering around the room nervously all the time, like she was looking for an escape route.

She caught up to Nathan on Friday afternoon after school, while he was walking home. She punched him playfully on the shoulder and smiled brightly, as if three days of them not speaking hadn't just gone by.

'How am I doing? Am I assimilating?'

'You're doing great. They seem to be responding well.'

'You make it sound like they're lab rats.'

He shrugged and they fell into silence. He didn't want her to stop smiling. He liked her best when she smiled.

He remembered when she'd first come to talk to him after class, in grade 8. It was a week after school had started and some of the kids were being really mean to him. His protective outer shell wasn't fully formed yet, so the nasty remarks sank in and bounced around his mind like echoes. Olivia had come up to him and introduced herself. He'd looked up and her smile was the first thing he'd noticed.

She'd twisted her plait between her fingers while she spoke, telling him that she was also having trouble adjusting, and that if he ever needed anyone to talk to, he could speak to her. He knew she was only being polite, which is why he didn't try and force his company on her. Back then, he was severely distrusting. But they'd remained friendly ever since.

Thankfully, her frown soon disappeared. 'So guess what? Jill asked me if I'm going to that party tonight.'

'That's good.'

'I know! And then she said she'll see me there.'

'Excellent.'

She beamed. 'And it's all because of you! But I keep forgetting what you told me and then I panic.'

'Why don't you read the notes you made, then?'

She laughed. 'I should, shouldn't I? I don't like taking the book out in class in case anyone sees it. You've made me paranoid after you saw my drawing.'

'Oh, I'm sorry. I didn't mean to.' He didn't like that he'd affected her negatively like that. He wanted to help her, not turn her into a mini version of himself. He turned this over in his mind, thinking of a way to reverse what he'd done.

'Nathan? You spaced out. What's happening?'

'Sorry, I was just thinking about what you said,' he spluttered, blinking at the ground as he tried to shirk the negative script running through his head.

'Please don't. I didn't mean anything by it. I was just joking.'

They came to a stop at an intersection. Her left foot pivoted on the toe. 'Look, I'll see you around, okay? I need to get some more tips from you. Hey, maybe I should just take your number?'

'Okay.' He didn't want the conversation to end there, but she was already rummaging in her satchel for her phone.

Say something, he thought. *Ask her what other plans she has for the weekend. Tell her an interesting fact about otters. Take down her number as well*. But the words stuck to the roof of his mouth like peanut butter. He knew what to say, but unlike Olivia, he couldn't follow through on his own advice.

'Bloody thing. Oh, here it is.' She typed in his number with her thumb, already backing away. 'Awesome. I'll be in touch, okay?'

'Okay. I'll try and come up with more advice or something.' Why did he say that? It was too late to take it back.

She smiled and walked briskly away.

He liked the way she walked. She lifted herself up on her toes with each step, almost like she was skipping. It was a happy walk that countered the sad expression she wore in class. Her behaviour and expressions constantly contradicted themselves like that: happy, sad, happy, sad. With his help, he hoped she would eventually settle on happy.

He didn't want to tell Mohendra about Olivia yet. It didn't seem right to. Mohendra spoke about girls like they were comic- book villains, always out to get him. So when Mohendra materialised in his doorway, the hood of his jacket pulled up over his peak cap, Nathan pushed all thoughts of Olivia to the furthest cor- ner of his mind.

'You won't believe it, but Karen has come over every day this week. She's clearly trying to tell me something.'

'Or maybe she's just visiting your sister,' Nathan suggested.

'You joke, but this girl is really doing something to me.'

Nathan imagined a red-headed version of the DC superhero Zatanna poking needles into a tiny Mohendra voodoo doll. 'Have you spoken to her?'

'A little,' said Mohendra, fiddling with his hands, suggesting he wasn't being altogether honest.

Nathan shifted his attention to Mohendra's laptop, and began plugging in network cables.

Wendy pushed open the door to say a quick hello before padding out, panting heavily.

'You see, even the lady dogs can't get enough of me,' laughed Mohendra, finally pulling down his hood and removing his cap.

'Bitches,' corrected Nathan automatically.

'Now, I wouldn't go that far, man.'

Nathan looked up, but Mohendra shook his head. 'Never mind, man. Never mind.'

Soon they were immersed in the game, trudging along the battleground and shooting everything in sight. All thoughts of Olivia and the temptress known as Karen disappeared as the action increased.

By the time they tired of the game, they'd reached T on Nathan's alphabetical playlist.

'How's it going, guys? Can I get you anything from the kitchen?' asked Nathan's dad, peeking in to check on them.

Mohendra looked at his watch. 'I'm just about to head home. I want to say good night to Karen before she leaves.'

'Do you need a lift?' asked Mr Langdon.

'Nah, I'll get an Uber to Wynberg Main Road and walk the rest of the way. It'll look better for me if I come home out of breath. Manly, you know? Cheers, Nathan.'

They watched him bolt out the room, his sneakers squeaking.

Nathan's dad came in and closed the door behind him. 'So what did you boys get up to tonight? You were very quiet. I didn't hear a peep out of you for hours.'

'We were playing Call of Duty. But it's getting boring.'

'You sound disappointed.'

'No, not really. We'll play something else next time. I'm thinking about hosting a modded Minecraft on my server.'

'Well, as long as you're keeping yourselves amused.'

Nathan looked up at his father curiously. The conversation didn't seem to have a point. He waited to see if there was anything else, but his father simply stood where he was. Nathan suspected his parents worried about him, and felt it their duty to ask after him every so often, but they needn't have bothered. He was fine.

'Well, I guess I should say good night, then,' said his dad eventually.

'Good night, Dad.'

When his father was gone, Nathan went online to see if Olivia was active on Instagram. He wasn't following anyone from school, and he didn't plan on changing that. He just wanted to look.

He found her profile easily. The picture was a happy one. She was outdoors somewhere. Judging by the silvery shimmer in the background, it was near the sea. She was smiling broadly and squinting slightly in the heavy sunlight. There weren't any privacy settings in place to stop him from looking at her information, which he found alarming. He would mention it to her casually in the morning. It was dangerous leaving all her private information open for the world to see. Nathan's profile was iron tight.

It bothered him that she was so careless about her privacy, but then no one else seemed to care about these things as much as he did.

6

Later that night, Nathan sat at his desk with a circuit board in front of him. He was building a robot, or at least trying to. Mohendra had sent him a YouTube link to an old TV show called *Robot Wars* on which contestants built their own robots to battle it out in a purpose-built arena. The tech was really old, but the show was entertaining enough.

Building something was a fun way to pass the rest of the night. Mohendra was supposed to be helping him, but Nathan didn't really mind. He preferred to work alone and without distraction. Knowing Mohendra, he would've spoken about his love life, or lack thereof, all night, making concentrating impossible.

Nathan enjoyed nothing better than tinkering. Building a robot catered to his innate desire to fix things. He wasn't good at the creative side, like adding decorations and weapons like they did on the show, but putting things together was as easy as building a puzzle. As a kid, he used to take the family's appliances apart, but he'd quickly learned that he got in less trouble if he built things from scratch. He was still everyone's go-to guy if the Wi-Fi went down though.

His phone buzzed on the table and he checked the message, expecting it to be from Mohendra, but it was from Olivia. *I'm all alone here. What am I supposed to do?*

He stared at the words for a long time before replying. *Pretend that you're having fun and try to find Jill or Blaize.*

He went back to work. In theory, the robot would work via infrared. He had to build a receiver, which required intense concentration.

His phone buzzed again. *She's talking to someone. I don't want to interrupt her. What should I do?*

He put down his screwdriver and picked up the phone. He typed, *Don't panic. Go get something to drink and go back when she's stopped talking.*

He'd just picked up his screwdriver when another message came through. *Can we chat so it looks like I'm busy on my phone?*

He stared at the wires and brackets before him and sighed. He would have to continue with his robot another time. He couldn't work if he was interrupted every five minutes. Besides, when his Raspberry Pi arrived from Takealot, he was probably going to start over anyway. *Are you having a good time?* he typed.

Not really.

But it's what you wanted.

That week, Olivia hadn't been able to keep her excitement contained. Nathan had never seen her so happy. He liked that he'd contributed to that. He didn't understand what had gone wrong, why she'd suddenly changed her mind.

When she didn't respond to his message he typed another. *Are you going to be okay?*

He waited, but he received no reply.

Olivia?

He stared at his phone for ages, and when she didn't reply, he assumed her phone had run out of battery. He knew he wasn't supposed to assume anything, but the alternative was worrying about a hundred different scenarios of Olivia in danger. It was easier to accept the simplest, least disturbing explanation.

He packed his tools and electronics away and changed into his pyjamas. It was too early to go to sleep, but he thought he might listen to music until he got tired. He'd just downloaded the latest Tool album.

His mother rapped on his door around midnight. 'Not too late tonight,' she called through the closed door.

'I'm already in bed, Mom.'

She opened the door and poked her head through. 'Oh, I see. Well, good night.'

'Good night, Mom.'

'I think you have a message on your phone,' she said before disappearing.

His head jerked to his bedside table. He'd put his phone on silent so as not to disturb his parents. He picked up the phone to read the message. *Nathan. Virginie is here. She's really cool. I'm dancing with her and her friends.*

His throat went dry. The mention of Virginie filled him with an inexplicable feeling of dread. He put the phone down and turned over on his pillow, but he couldn't get comfortable. He felt suddenly guilty about coaching Olivia. She wasn't like those girls, who laughed at the expense of others. She was a good person. No amount of pretending could hide that.

He turned over onto his other side. He hadn't factored in that aggression and social status were linked. Those with the most social connections were more aggressive. They'd protect their social status no matter what. Virginie was the most popular girl at school. That meant she was the most dangerous.

He sat up and reached for his phone again. There were no new messages on WhatsApp. He waited in the quiet dark, his mind racing. He imagined that they were being mean to Olivia or humiliating her at the party in front of all the popular kids from school. She would change schools for sure and then he'd never see her again.

The air suddenly seemed too thin. It would be impossible to sleep.

7

Nathan shook his head as he walked, trying to dislodge the thoughts that plagued him. He'd sent Olivia several messages over the course of the weekend, but she'd sent him only a single text: *I'm fine. Chill out.*

This only distressed him more. 'I'm fine' could mean a hundred different things. He'd learned that when someone said they were fine, it usually meant that they weren't fine, but how could he make such an assumption without seeing her face? What if 'fine' simply meant just that, that she was fine?

He opened and closed his hands, another nervous motion. He walked faster, making his backpack bounce uncomfortably on his back. He was doubly flustered because his agitation had caused an argument with his mother, who'd thought he was having 'one of his moods'. It was pointless trying to explain to her what was bothering him. He would never be her normal teenage son, Nathan. Not when her mind was being constantly poisoned by anti-vaxxer nonsense. Anything and everything he did was dissected. It made talking to her impossible. He quickened his pace before he got caught in the rain.

When he reached school, he didn't try to slip into invisibility, but rather forced himself through the stream of oncoming students, pushing past those who stood chatting in the middle of the passage. Some, mostly girls, glared at him; others responded more aggressively and pushed him back. He ignored them and pushed on, ignoring the loud, angry voices demanding he come back.

He stopped at the entrance to the cafeteria. Olivia was standing at the edge of the group of girls. She was smiling, laughing with them. Her hair was once again pulled into a messy bun, with strands of black hair escaping around her face. She'd succeeded in winning them over, then.

Still, he couldn't dismiss the thought that there was something off about the scene. She was still different from them. Her straight-backed posture hinted at ill-disguised panic.

The other girls were also far from relaxed. Their body language told him a story. They circled the slender Virginie in the centre, protecting her. The way they huddled together around their leader, the way they all stared expectantly at the newcomer, was almost predatory, like pack animals. Olivia, whose hands kept returning to a loose strand of hair, was oblivious to the danger.

Nathan hesitated. He wanted to rush to her side, to pull her away from the group of girls, but he knew that people didn't do that sort of thing in school. He'd be that crazy autistic kid again, mumbling something ridiculous about pack animals, alienating them both. He turned away reluctantly and made his way to class.

He wished he could switch off his brain sometimes.

He was conscious throughout the day of how upset he was. The worst of it was in mathematics, when he found that he couldn't follow the lesson. This had never happened before. Numbers were a language he could understand, that he found comfort in. They were the notes that fell into place on the music sheet of his mind, that created something exquisite. But sitting in class, staring at the stick figures on the whiteboard created nothing in his mind but noise. The machine that was his brain was broken.

Instead of solving the maths problem, his thoughts were once again on Olivia. This is what she'd wanted. If he said anything now, she'd either distrust his words or, worse, believe him and become sad all over again.

He groaned and dropped his head into his hands. He always hated that sad look on her face, so much so that he treasured the times she did smile.

'Nathan, are you alright? Do you want to go to the nurse?'

Nathan looked up and into the eyes of his maths teacher, Mr Nicholson, who was kneeling at his desk in concern. He was what Mohendra would call a ginger. Even his eyebrows were orange.

'I'm okay. I've just got a headache,' he said, which was technically true.

He stiffened as Mr Nicholson put a hand on his back. 'If you need to go home, I can write you a note.'

It was the same patronising tone Mr Wright has used. Suddenly, Mr Nicholson was no longer Nathan's favourite teacher.

He shook his head. 'I'm okay.'

'Okay. Just shout if you change your mind.'

Mr Nicholson eased himself back to his feet and returned to the front of the class, but not before patting Nathan on the back one last time. He flinched involuntarily.

He picked up his pen and started mechanically copying down sums. The answers to the algebra problems were already hovering there, waiting for him to write them down. So his mind wasn't broken after all. It was simply a case of some problems being more important than mathematics.

It had stopped raining, so at lunchtime he watched from his position under the tree as Olivia was introduced to everyone in the group. There were plenty of 'Oh, hi's and 'Oh my god's and typical teenage-girl giggles.

Olivia was beaming, her smile big and natural. He could hear the sound of her laughter above that of the others. Hers was the sweetest.

He knew he should be happy for her, but he couldn't ignore what was right in front of him. The scene was wrong. They were acting. He took a bite of his cheese-and-tomato sandwich and studied them. Usually the soggy texture caused by the tomato vexed him to no end, but today he tolerated it, instead focusing on the scene in front of him. Virginie wore a subtle smile that could easily be mistaken as a smirk by the little upturn at the corners of her mouth. She wouldn't be smirking unless she had something planned.

Nathan's mind continued to reel. He remembered when Virginie had sat behind him in geography class. For tests, their teacher preferred for students to say the answers out loud, instead of handing in a test paper. One of Virginie's friends had leaned over Nathan's shoulder to copy down his answers, then passed them to Virginie. They hadn't even tried to hide what they were doing and somehow had got away with it. Virginie had raised her hand for each answer, and each time she answered correctly, she was praised for it. She'd worn the same smirk then.

Nathan's fingers scrambled inside his lunchbox, but it was empty. He hadn't even realised he'd moved on to the other half of his sandwich. He looked at his watch. There were still ten minutes before the bell rang. For the first time in his high-school career, he wished he had someone to share break with, for some idle conversation to distract him from his thoughts.

He had no choice but to sit with his back against the tree and wait. At one point his eyes met Olivia's, and she smiled. He smiled too. He couldn't help it.

When the bell rang she hovered behind, under the pretence of looking for something in her bag. When Nathan walked past, she stood up, and skipped the short distance between them. 'Nathan, wait.'

He waited for her to catch up. 'Hi, Olivia.'

'Your advice worked,' she said, grinning.

'I see so,' he replied drily.

Her shoulders slumped. He wondered if she knew how tense her body had been up to that point. 'They're actually really nice,' she said.

'I never said they weren't.' *But he should have.*

'I know. I guess I always imagined they were bitchy, but they're really cool. Thanks for helping me.'

He nodded, knowing he should say something more. He'd been lying awake most of the weekend, had been obsessing

51

about her situation all day. This was the moment he'd been waiting for, but the words wouldn't come out.

She grinned at him, and her arms flopped at her sides. He'd just started wondering what that was about when he found himself enveloped in a hug. He closed his eyes as the smell of her hair flooded his senses. It smelled like vanilla. He could taste it in his mouth, like the custard his mother made at Christmas. When she pulled away, he was surprised to see that her cheeks were blotchy.

'I ... er, bye.'

She turned and walked briskly away.

He stayed where he was until the last of her scent had disappeared in the breeze.

8

Mohendra stared at Nathan in surprise. Nathan usually spoke only when he had something important to say, but suddenly he couldn't stop talking. Mohendra sat back as the flood of words overwhelmed him. His laptop case remained unopened on his lap.

Nathan flailed his hands. 'I should have said something. Why didn't I say anything?' His legs bounced uncontrollably.

Mohendra cleared his throat. He'd tried, unsuccessfully, to interrupt Nathan's ranting a few times. 'I don't understand. Are you sure those girls are really up to something? You're not the best judge of character, man.'

'What's that supposed to mean?'

'Well, you don't trust anybody.'

Nathan snorted. 'That's only a general rule. Usually people can't be trusted unless they prove otherwise, but this situation is different. Olivia doesn't know what's coming. And you said it yourself: girls can't be trusted.'

'I know, but how do you know? And how much do you

actually know about Olivia? She's a girl too, you know. She probably has her own secret plans. How do you know you can trust her? It sounds to me like she used you to get in with that group. If anything, she deserves what's coming.'

Nathan felt the heat rise in his cheeks. 'Olivia isn't like other girls. She wouldn't do that.'

'Nathan, you don't have experience with any girls. How would you know the difference?'

Nathan thought carefully about his friend's words. He recalled all his memories of Olivia, their brief encounters since that first day she'd extended her hand in friendship, the way she looked at the ground when people spoke to her, just like he did, her loneliness, her sadness. 'She's different,' he said eventually.

Mohendra nodded. 'Maybe you should wait and see what happens. If those girls are as evil as you say, then they're going to show it at some point. You might be freaking out for nothing.'

'What about Olivia? I have to warn her.'

'No, you don't. She won't listen. Trust me. Let her find out for herself.'

Nathan flopped down on the bed, making the springs squeal. 'This is all my fault. I shouldn't have said anything to begin with. What was I thinking?'

'It sounds like you're in love with this Olivia.'

Nathan sat up and stared at Mohendra in surprise. 'What? Where did that come from?'

'You're acting like a man in love.'

'Am I?'

Love was a topic that Nathan had given very little thought to. The word hung in the air like the echoes of a police siren, ringing in his ears. 'How would I know if I was in love?'

It was an awkward question, but he really needed to know. If anyone could tell him, it was Mohendra. He fell in love at least twice a month.

Thankfully, Mohendra was used to his bluntness. He chewed the inside of his cheeks as he considered the question. 'Do you think about her all the time? I mean all the time, like nothing else can get into your brain while she's there?'

'Yes.'

He didn't hesitate. 'Then I think you're in love, man.'

'Oh.'

This explained everything – why his day revolved around her movements, why he'd had no control over his own mind for the last few days. It was completely overwhelming. 'What do I do?' he asked.

Mohendra shrugged. 'I have no idea.'

They sat in silence for a while. They were in foreign territory when it came to love. The thought of playing computer games was too easy a way out of continuing the conversation. Too obvious. Instead, they sat helplessly, occasionally glancing at each other while the silence lengthened.

Nathan knew that Mohendra had never had an official girlfriend, so most of what he said was theory, but still, this conclusion felt right. He was in love with Olivia February. Was she the girl of his dreams, as the expression went? He considered this. He'd never dreamed of her, but he did think about her a lot.

She was beautiful, that was true, although it wasn't something he thought about often. She was just Olivia. He imagined them as a couple and decided that he enjoyed her company enough to want to spend more time with her. And he actually liked it when she touched him.

Wendy's paws click-clacked across the tiles several times as she passed the room, confused by the unnatural silence.

Eventually, Nathan said out loud what was bothering him even more than the sudden realisation that he was in love. 'What if she doesn't love me back?'

Mohendra bowed his head. 'I've never had a girl like me back,' he admitted.

'What's that like?'

Mohendra shrugged. 'It hurts for a bit, but you get used to it. It hasn't stopped me from trying again.'

Nathan nodded. He was so used to people treating him as sub-human that he wasn't affected by it any more. But if it came from Olivia, he suspected it might feel different. He stared down at his hands. 'I don't think she loves me back. Not if I'm like this.'

'What do you mean? You're fine.'

Nathan shook his head. 'I don't even like me like this.' It was something he'd never admitted before.

Mohendra started unpacking his laptop. 'You're being stupid now, man. You never had a problem before this girl came along. Let's just play a game.'

Nathan opened his Alienware machine, but he was thinking that Mohendra was wrong. The truth was that he was incredibly frustrated by how others perceived him. He accepted that that was the reality of being on the spectrum. He looked just like everyone else, but when he opened his mouth, he was different. People's eyes glazed over when he talked, their smiles disappeared, they treated him differently.

But he'd helped Olivia to change. He let the thought rest in his mind while he logged in to Steam. It was there while he ran down the dusty streets of Sarajevo, gun at the ready. It was there when Mohendra couldn't contain his yawns any more and said a sleepy goodbye. It was there when his father came home from work after another late day in court.

He sat down on a barstool at the marble table while his dad heated up his cottage pie and peas, his tie hanging loosely around his neck.

'Dad, do you think it's possible to change the perception people have of you by adjusting your own behaviour?'

His father put down his knife and fork and stared at his son in bewilderment. 'Do you know, I still get surprised by some of the things you say. You would've thought that after fifteen years, I'd have got used to it by now.'

Nathan shrugged and, ignoring what his father had said, continued. 'You're a lawyer. You must meet tons of people trying to pretend they're something they're not.'

His father nodded. 'Well, I do see a lot of people trying to act innocent, often unconvincingly.'

'What are they doing wrong?'

Nathan's father smiled at him warmly. 'It's usually little things that give them away, like smiling and trying to hide it, or shifting their gaze for a split-second when they tell a lie.'

Nathan nodded. Micro expressions. He already knew about those.

'Dare I ask why you're suddenly interested in behaviour modification?' asked his father, a forkful of mince halfway to his mouth.

'I'm helping someone change the way other people look at them.'

His father gave him a knowing look. 'Do you think it will work?'

'Yes.' A hint of doubt flickered somewhere in the back of his mind, but he shrugged the thought away. There were many variables involved, but he was smart enough to work them all out. He nodded to himself. *Yes, it will work.*

He left his father staring after him, even more befuddled than before. Nathan suspected that his dad had seen right through his little duplicity, but he wouldn't say anything.

Nathan wasn't very good at lying to people, which is why he simply rephrased the truth so that it sounded different. He would use the same reasoning to transform himself. If it meant having Olivia as his girlfriend, he had to try. He had nothing to lose.

9

To achieve his goal, Nathan made a list of things to concentrate on while he was at school.

1. Posture
2. Confidence
3. Eye contact
4. Friendliness
5. Assertiveness

The goal was to appear normal, to assimilate with the rest of his class. That meant no more shying away from people, no mumbling, no staring at the ground while he walked.

Standing up straight all the time proved to be challenging, but Nathan was determined to try. Another thing he found hard to stop was apologising every time someone walked into him. Normal teenagers reacted in two ways: aggressive or friendly. He would try the latter and see how that worked.

It was terrifying to shrug off the invisible force field he'd spent years perfecting, but he had to do this. Now that the idea of winning over Olivia was firmly implanted in his brain, nothing felt more important.

The first he saw of her was in the hallways between classes. Olivia had become a part of the group of girls who travelled to class as one inseparable flock. She was like them in every detail, from her hair, to her posture, to her laugh. But while the other girls in the group mirrored Virginie, Olivia still retained her Olivia-ness. She had her own unique spark that could never diminish.

While they walked past, a cluster of identical girls, Nathan only saw one face among them. She smiled and he smiled in return. She looked back at him curiously as she passed, as if having suddenly noticed something different about him.

For the first time since they'd known each other, he'd maintained eye contact with her. It was an unbearable few seconds of not blinking.

Later that afternoon Olivia was at the door. Nathan stared at her in wonder. With the exception of Mohendra, he'd never had anyone over, least of all a girl.

'Hello,' she said. 'I didn't get to talk to you at school, so I thought I'd come over.'

Because that's not weird.

'Um, okay. Sure.'

He felt faint and his hands trembled in his pockets as he led Olivia to his room. His mother goggled at them from the lounge. Nathan suspected that as soon as his door closed, she'd run to call his father to tell him the news.

Was he allowed to have his door closed if he had a girl over?

He stood in the doorway and motioned for her to go first. 'Do you want some tea or something?'

'Blech, no. I hate tea. Sit down. I have a lot to tell you.' Olivia jumped onto his bed and bounced up and down. 'So Virginie is having a party for her birthday at the end of the month. She was telling everyone about how her father is going to hire a famous DJ and have the pool surrounded by coloured lights. It's going to be massive.'

'Did she invite you?'

'I'm getting there! Don't rush me.'

'Okay, okay.'

Nathan sat down in his gaming chair while Olivia rattled on about the day's highlights among her new tribe. It was a shock having her there, but her presence made sense. It was impossible for them to speak at school – she was always with her pack, during class, between class, at break.

His room felt different with Olivia in it; smaller. Or maybe it was because he was finding it harder to breathe with her in it.

'So yes. She invited me personally. It was so scary. She has this dreamy soft voice and you have to lean forward to listen.'

'That's great.' *So why were his insides squirming at the thought?*

'I know! I couldn't believe it. I felt so special. She's very shy, actually.'

'Uh huh.' *No, she's calculating.*

Olivia stopped talking to look around his room. The sight of her large brown eyes taking in his stuff made him inhale sharply. Every aspect of his life was on display. What would she think? Was she secretly judging him? Did he care?

She pointed to the pile of electronic equipment on his desk. 'What's that?'

'I'm building a robot.'

'That's so cool! I knew you were smart, but I didn't know you were that smart.'

'Thanks.' He thought it was really easy to build a robot, but she might take offence if he said that out loud. He didn't want her to think that he thought less of her in any way.

Olivia picked up one of his graphic novels and pried it out of its plastic envelope. She licked her finger before turning the page. Nathan cringed, but resisted the urge to grab it out of her hands. Her eyes glanced over the pictures. 'This is so awesome,' she said. 'Do you collect comics?'

'I collect graphic novels,' he corrected.

'Ah, I see. They're thicker.'

He wanted to laugh at how sure she sounded about it, but that would be rude. 'They're usually thicker, yes,' he said, phrasing the words carefully.

She beamed at him and carefully put down the graphic novel. Her eyes scanned the rest of the room, lingering on the collectable vinyl figures that stood in a line on his shelf – his 'toys', as his mother called them. 'I like your room,' she said eventually.

'I like it too.'

She laughed, but her smile quickly faded. 'Is it weird that I have this ball of fear inside me all the time?'

He shifted his weight in his chair. She was confusing him by switching moods all the time, and it unnerved him. It was hard to concentrate on being normal if she was being the complete opposite. It was hard enough being around her when she was smiling.

'What are you afraid of?' he asked.

'I'm not sure. Do you think it's one of those unconscious things you told me about? Maybe I'm afraid they're going to find out that I'm a huge faker.'

'You're not a faker. Just because you're conscious of what you're saying and how you're saying it doesn't change who you are. You're still the same Olivia.'

'I suppose so, but no one liked that version of me.'

'I did.'

They both turned as Nathan's door inched open. His mother appeared in the doorway, smiling strangely. 'Anyone want tea?' she asked. Her voice was unusually cheerful.

Olivia looked up and swiped a strand of hair from her face. 'No, thank you, Mrs Langdon.'

Nathan's mother smiled broadly. 'I didn't get your name, dear.'

'It's Olivia. Olivia February.'

Nathan watched his mother warily. She was definitely snooping. She hovered in the doorway and looked around the room like she was trying to work out what they'd been doing before she entered. 'Are you two in the same class?'

Olivia nodded. 'Most classes. Except geography.'

His mother's smile never faltered. 'Is Nathan helping you with your homework?'

Olivia blinked in surprise. 'No. I'm just visiting.'

'Oh, of course. I'll leave you to it, then.'

When she was gone, Olivia turned back to Nathan. 'Your mom's nice.'

'She can be.'

Her face morphed again, this time into an expression he couldn't understand, possibly confusion. He bit his lip, fighting the racing thoughts rising up from the back of his mind. He had to keep his composure, but it had become infinitely harder. 'Can you say something please? I can't tell what you're thinking.' He hated that he had to ask her, but it was maddening not knowing what was on her mind.

She laughed. 'Oh, Nathan. What were we talking about again?'

That I liked you the way you were before.

'About you not being a faker.'

'Oh, ja.' Her face screwed up into a frown.

He resisted the urge to lean across and move a strand of hair out of her face. Instead, he did it ten times in his mind, each time resulting in a different response. Her recoiling out the way, her blushing, her leaning forward to make it easier to reach her …

'You're staring into space again.'

'What?' He didn't even know he'd been doing it.

She had the most expressive face he'd ever seen. In an hour, her features had transformed from happy to sad, confused to excited, tired to bored, and then back to happy again. She was all the seasons in one, fascinating but also utterly bewildering. He could stare at her forever. Her eyes changed colour. Sometimes they were darker, sometimes bright with hidden fire. He could tell when she was thinking because her nose would scrunch up and she'd look up. Always up.

'What can I do to make sure they don't figure me out?' she asked.

Stay away from them.

'Don't show any fear. As long as you continue to blend in, they shouldn't have any reason to turn on you. Act natural.'

'Those are just words. What can I actually *do* to make them really like me for real?'

He sifted through the information in his mind, ignoring the desire to tell her to run away before it was too late. 'If someone talks to you, take an interest in what they're saying and try to remember the details. Ask them about it when you see them again. You'll come across as thoughtful.'

She laughed. 'I like to think that I'm already thoughtful.'

He shrugged. 'Then it won't be hard for you. Just be their friend, like you are with me.'

She stuck out her tongue and shifted towards his laptop, opening the lid. 'Do you have any music?'

He resisted the urge to pull the laptop away from her. 'Spotify should be open already. Just click play.'

She pouted in concentration as she tried to navigate using the trackpad. 'Where's your mouse?'

'I don't use one.'

She gave him an incredulous look, the same one his mother wore when she wanted to look something up on the internet. He was getting better at reading people.

The soft electronic compilation tinkled though the machine's built-in speakers. Her head swayed in time to the rhythm.

'I like having friends,' she said, eventually. 'And yes, that includes you. You're my best friend.'

Her words derailed him, filling him with guilt and making his thoughts speed up to 120 kilometres an hour. His carefully controlled composure began to unravel. He felt his back slouch, and his fingers began to scramble for something to fiddle with. His leg started to bounce.

She laughed at his discomfort, and suddenly all of Mohendra's dire warnings about girls made sense. She was playing him like a child with putty, reshaping him for her own amusement.

'Stop it,' he said.

'Oh, Nathan. There you go, making me laugh again.'

His mouth opened in surprise. What was this girl doing to him?

She dived onto her stomach, messing up the duvet. 'Ooh, I have an idea. Why don't you come otter-spotting with me this weekend?'

He looked up in surprise. 'Um, what?' The question had come out of nowhere.

'Otter-spotting. It's where you go looking for otters in the river. It's fun.'

He was still stunned, but he managed to pull himself together. 'What do you do with the otters when you find them?'

'Nothing. You just look at them. It's awesome. I'm sure you'll love it.'

Nathan nodded. Talking to Mohendra or his gaming buddies was easy. They usually stuck to certain topics and never deviated. With Olivia, he never knew what she was going to say next.

'Okay.'

'Okay!' she beamed.

She disappeared as quickly as she had come, with the promise that he would meet her at the Liesbeek River near Mowbray that Saturday morning. His head was in such a spin that his hands shook when he closed the door behind her.

During dinner Nathan tried his best to field his parents' questions. He had no doubt that his father already knew about Olivia's visit. He'd mysteriously come home early, which had instantly aroused Nathan's suspicion.

His mother smiled at his dad. 'We had a visitor today,' she said.

'Oh, yes?'

And so it began.

'Yes, a pretty girl named Olivia something-or-other.'

'Olivia February,' said Nathan.

His father put down his cutlery and folded his hands into a steeple shape. 'A girl from school?'

'Yes. She's my friend.'

'That's wonderful. Were you helping her with her homework?'

Nathan rolled his eyes. 'No. Why do you both assume that? You tell me not to make assumptions all the time. Is it so hard to think of me having other friends?'

'Alright, Nathan, calm down,' said his mom.

His parents shared a look. It really annoyed him when they did that. 'Don't do that,' he said, realising too late that his voice had risen.

'Sorry,' said his dad, raising both hands placatingly.

Nathan was becoming upset at the way things were escalating. The familiar roar of carefully compartmentalised thoughts escaping into a building storm made him clutch the sides of his head. It had been a long time since he'd lost his composure.

His parents watched him warily. 'Nathan? Is everything alright?' asked his dad.

Nathan kept his head in his hands until the noise stopped.

He couldn't think straight. Olivia's visit had been the trigger. It had been completely unexpected, and unexpected things shook his brain around like someone shaking a wrapped box to try to guess what was inside. Couldn't they see that? If only his parents would just understand him.

When the maelstrom passed, he pushed his plate away and stood up, still disoriented and a little anxious. 'Why can't you just be normal around me? Why does it always feel like you're just waiting for me to explode?'

His mom reached across to place her hand over his. 'We're sorry,' she said.

If only her expression matched her tone.

About half an hour later, his dad entered his room while Nathan was playing DOTA online, and took a seat on the edge of the bed. 'Why don't you tell me about Olivia? I've only got your mother's take on it so far.'

Nathan's eyes didn't leave the screen. 'Why is it so important?'

'Your mother seems to think it is.'

'Olivia is a friend. I've told you this twice now.'

'Come on, kid. Talk to me. I'm interested in this stuff.'

On the screen, Nathan's warrior flickered out of existence in a rain of spells. He looked up and spoke quickly to get it all out in one go. 'Olivia is a girl in my class. She's not taking advantage of me or getting me to do her homework. She's really nice.'

'So when you asked me the other night about changing people's perceptions, I'm guessing this had something to do with Olivia?'

Nathan switched off the screen, but he didn't turn around from his desk. He'd been so careful to conceal his meaning, but his father was a lot more perceptive than he'd given him credit for. 'I don't think she could ever like me the way I am now.'

'But she came to visit you today.'

'So? What has that got to do with it?'

'Sounds to me like she already likes you.'

Nathan looked up in amazement, but didn't turn around. He heard the rustling of his bedcovers, telling him his father had risen to leave.

'Don't tell Mom, okay?'

His father hesitated by the door. 'Sure, kid. It's guy stuff. I get it.'

What if his dad was right? The revelation was like a lightning bolt surging through him.

Nathan was relatively happy. School presented no difficulty. Life at home was manageable. Mohendra was there if he ever needed company, or he could just lose a couple of hours gaming. He'd never questioned his life before.

Now that Olivia was there, everything had suddenly changed. Everything before seemed inadequate in comparison. It suddenly needed her in it.

This made no sense. He'd never needed people before. It baffled him that his entire way of thinking had shifted so quickly.

She was doing something to him that he didn't understand.

10

From a quick internet search, Nathan discovered that the Cape clawless otter was a rare creature. Sightings were so uncommon that there were blogs devoted to the subject, and amateur otter-spotters were encouraged to post pictures of their sightings online. Olivia called it 'otter madness'.

On a chilly, grey Saturday morning, Nathan's dad dropped him on the bank of the Liesbeek River where it skirted the M5 highway, a ribbon of green between the highway and the suburbs. A pair of fishermen in blue overalls were starting to set up for the day near the water. From this vantage point, Nathan had a good view of Table Mountain. Puffy white clouds billowed down the slopes into the suburbs below.

'Are you sure you'll be safe?' his father asked.

Nathan shrugged. 'How am I supposed to know? I'm not psychic.'

'Alright, Nathan. No need to be cheeky. Just look after yourself.'

Nathan watched as his dad re-entered the traffic flow, the car behind him hooting angrily, then went off in search of Olivia. It was light enough so it didn't take long to find her. She was wading through the mulch in dark-green wellington boots. Her checked shirt was rolled up to the elbows, and her cut-off jeans were already splattered in mud.

'Hey, Olivia,' he called.

She turned around slowly and waved, but stopped when she took in his appearance. 'Don't tell me you're wearing that?'

He looked down at his clothes. He was wearing a pair of blue jeans, sneakers and a black T-shirt. He didn't have anything else to wear. He'd never been otter-spotting before. 'I'll roll up my jeans,' he said.

She rolled her eyes. 'Well, hurry up. They'll disappear as soon as the sun gets too bright.'

He bent down to roll up his jeans, exposing his pale, skinny shins, before joining Olivia further down the bank. She stood with her legs apart, feet planted firmly in the mud, and stared down into the brown water.

'How do you know they're in there?' he asked.

'Because I've seen one before,' she replied matter-of-factly, like it was obvious. She added, 'Wherever you find freshwater crabs, you'll find otters. It's their favourite food.'

Nodding, he slipped and slid his way to where she was standing. He didn't remove his shoes in case of broken glass, and it only took three steps for his shoes and socks to become drenched. He didn't own a pair of wellington boots because he'd never had need of them.

A thin mist travelled across the river, dampening their skin.

'The crabs enter the Liesbeek River from the streams that flow through Kirstenbosch Gardens,' he said absently.

She turned around sharply. 'How do you know that?'

He shrugged. 'I looked it up online last night.'

'Oh.' She seemed disappointed that it wasn't something he just knew by heart.

The mist made her hair stick to her neck and face, but she was oblivious to it. With her arms outstretched, she tightrope-walked her way to the very edge of the riverbank.

Nathan wanted to reach out and take her hand so that she didn't fall. He went as far as to move his arm towards her, then pulled it back. He moved slowly after her, and lowered himself down onto his haunches so that he could keep two hands on the ground as he skidded down the bank.

Olivia was concentrating so hard on the surface of the water that she didn't even notice him struggling to reach her. 'The first time I saw an otter was with my dad,' she said, keeping her eyes on the water. 'We were at a restaurant in St James, and this creature just ran in under the tables. The owner thought it was a rat, but its body was too flat. Everyone had to wait outside until the SPCA came to get it. When they brought it out, wriggling like crazy, it was the cutest thing I'd ever seen.'

'What happened to it?' he asked.

'They released the poor guy into a vlei, but let me finish my story! Otter-spotting has become a hobby now. I've even seen them at Kirstenbosch Gardens, which is really rare.'

Nathan smiled. Being out in the cold early morning with wet socks wasn't his idea of fun, but it was nice to discover a different layer to Olivia. Olivia the otter-spotter. It fitted. The more time he spent with her, the more was revealed.

He supposed Olivia-spotting was his hobby. He needed to watch her more carefully to see if he could discover any telltale signs that she liked him. He wanted to believe it was true, but it would be naive to get his hopes up too early. He needed to be sure. And that would require all the observational skills he had in his arsenal.

They sat on the bank and watched the muddy water curl and fold across the rocks. Traffic built up on the road behind them, but it was a different world to theirs. In theirs, an ibis waded in the shallows, piercing the mud with its black needle beak, searching for the delicacies that existed below the surface. Beyond the ibis, the tall brown reeds shuddered in the wind, whispering softly. Table Mountain watched silently over everything.

Nathan sat back and tried to relax, which was incredibly difficult with Olivia so close. To calm himself, he studied their surroundings. He could just make out the top of the observatory above the trees.

A movement beside him drew him back. Olivia yanked out a reed and began twirling it between her fingers. 'I haven't been here in ages,' she said.

'Do you come here with your dad?'

She tossed the reed into the brown water. 'No. He took off.'

'When he comes back, then?'

'I don't think he's coming back, Nathan. He's been gone three years already. It's just me, my ma and my grandmother now.'

'I'm sorry.'

'It's okay. I think he has another family or something. That's what my ma says.'

Nathan couldn't come up with a single thing to say to that. He wanted to talk about something happier, not missing fathers and other sad facts of life. He and Mohendra often discussed superheroes and made up various scenarios to gauge who would win, but he didn't think Olivia would be into that. But he would have to wait until she decided to speak again.

They sat in silence and watched the river birds drift past. When he looked up, she was staring at him.

'You didn't move your lips when you spaced out just then,' she said.

'Oh, I've been working on it.'

'Now you just look cute when you stare,' she said.

He turned away, willing his cheeks not to blush.

'Have I changed?' she asked, shifting closer to him. 'You haven't really told me how I'm doing.'

He forced himself to meet her eyes. 'Oh, um ... You're assimilating really well. They seem to have accepted you.'

She grinned. 'You make it sound like we're playing spies and you're training me how to infiltrate enemy lines.'

'I didn't say that.'

'Yes, but you know what I mean.'

He really, really wished she would stop using that phrase. If he knew what she meant, he wouldn't misunderstand her all the time.

After they'd been sitting for what felt like hours, and the mist had lifted to reveal a silvery sheen on the water's surface, Olivia sprang up and squealed. 'There's one. Over there!'

Nathan looked to where she'd pointed. All he could see was a ripple in the water. 'Are you sure it wasn't just an egret or something?'

'No, it wasn't a bloody egret, Nathan!' Olivia covered her mouth with her hand. Nathan deducted that it was a gesture of excitement. Either that or fear, but fear didn't fit the situation.

He stared at the shimmering surface of the water, but the otter, if that's what it had been, didn't reappear. 'Do you have a logbook that you record the date and time in?'

She looked at him blankly. 'What? No. I suppose I should do that, shouldn't I?'

Her words were defensive. He wondered if she was embarrassed. 'It's what I would do if I was into otter-spotting. Or build an app.'

She frowned.

Great going, Nathan.

'You don't have to have a logbook, though,' he added hurriedly. 'I'm sure lots of people go otter-spotting without one.'

Her smile returned and his panic receded a little. No damage done.

Olivia was determined to look on, but she didn't spot any more otters. They moved all the way up the bank, passing a small flock of soft-pink flamingos relaxing in the shallows.

That one near-glimpse had been enough for Nathan. It had been a perfect day. Even if it had been a mad, spontaneous idea, he was happier than he'd been in a long time. Olivia thought he was cute.

He'd been hoping for a sign, and she'd presented one to him freely.

11

There were seven letters in the name 'Othello'. Eighteen in 'William Shakespeare'. There were three hundred and twenty pages in the textbook.

Nathan couldn't stop. He tried to breathe but his chest had become a locked safe that wouldn't allow any more air in or out. Just what he needed: a panic attack.

He forced himself to breathe deeply through his nose. His breathing was shallow at first, and his lungs felt like they were full of Rice Krispies. He closed his eyes and concentrated on the simple act of inhaling and exhaling, ignoring the raucous noise in his head.

One hundred, ninety-nine, ninety-eight, ninety-seven ...

Nathan waited for the world to stop spinning. He rubbed his temples vigorously, but the panic wasn't subsiding. It didn't help that he was in the middle of English class. He imagined himself standing up, picking up his bag and walking out. He wouldn't stop walking until he was out the school gates, past the watchful eyes of the teachers and prefects, until he'd reached an open field where he could bellow until all the frustration was purged from his body.

He opened his eyes and he was back in the frenetic classroom, full of whispers and concealed laughter and the scrape of chairs. Mrs Booysen banged her hand on her desk to try and get everyone's attention.

Nathan closed his eyes again. His headache was deep inside his head, too deep for his fingers to reach. He'd worked himself up to that point by worrying too much about the possible repercussions of helping Olivia become popular. He'd been thinking about it all night. Doubts scratched at him with otter claws. Too many things could go wrong. He hadn't thought the strategy through well enough.

Olivia gave him a worried look from the front of the class. Next to her, one of her new friends, the aggressive Mandy, nudged her elbow into Olivia's side and laughed. Mandy was laughing at him because he was being weird again.

Olivia didn't laugh, though. She smiled like he'd taught her to do, and turned back to the front. Mandy frowned at Olivia and slumped back into her chair, clearly disappointed that her new friend hadn't laughed too. But Nathan had known she wouldn't. She kept proving over and over again that she wasn't like them. That was the problem.

She was too good for them. They kept showing themselves for who they really were, but how did he know that wasn't his own distrustful mind looking for signs to be suspicious of? Why was it so difficult for him to see them as normal teenage girls?

He shook his head to try and dislodge the thought. He told himself that there was no such thing as a normal teenage girl. Everyone was capable of cruelty. It was a default setting for most humans. And group thinking brought it out. He rested his head against the cool wooden desk covered in years of pen scrawl. Why did he care so much about this?

When the bell eventually rang, he grabbed his bag and scrambled out of class before anyone else. Instead of heading for his next class, he walked straight to the entrance, and out through the double doors. He needed space and air.

Nathan had never bunked school before. He got a strange sensation from it, a small sense of exhilaration. He was breaking routine, which was a lot more satisfying than sitting at his desk all day, thinking the same thoughts over and over. There was no field nearby where he could scream till his throat hurt. Instead, he retraced his morning's steps back to his house, which was, thankfully, deserted, with his parents both at work.

He let himself in and walked to his room, depositing his backpack on the floor and slinging his blazer over the back of his gaming chair. His heart was still beating too fast. He needed to concentrate on something that required the use of both his head and his hands.

He sat down at his desk and let his mind zone out. Building robots wasn't simply a matter of electronics and circuitry, it was about mathematics. For the leg configuration, he used equations to work out the torque at each joint. His calculations had to be exact so that the robot didn't fall over when it moved. The figures circled his mind. He had to take into account the weight of the robot, and the weight of the legs, forces such as movement, stability, normal force and torque balance. Each element had a value and was represented by a specific symbol. He made some notes on a piece of paper, lines and lines of numbers and letters that created a complicated equation that had to be followed exactly.

All the thoughts that plagued him dissolved into the background. There was no space for anything but the calculations. Once in a while he'd check something on the troubleshooting forums online, then he bent back to the task. The body was starting to take shape. The legs were evenly apart. He would still need to design and attach the rotor before testing it out.

Nathan nodded to himself, made more notes on the paper that was covered in his untidy handwriting. It was so full that he had to turn it over and start on the other side.

He didn't notice the shadows lengthening around him.

A knock on his bedroom door made him sit up straight in surprise. He'd thought he was alone at home, but the door opened and his mother's face appeared.

She scanned the room. 'You've been very quiet.'

'When did you get home?' Nathan asked her bluntly.

'Um, about an hour ago. It's almost time for dinner. Are you going to come set the table?'

Nathan's eyes swivelled to the time at the bottom right-hand side of his laptop. It was nearly seven in the evening. He'd been busy for six hours.

'Okay, sure,' he said absently.

Neither of his parents asked him why he'd bunked school. His absence had evidently gone unnoticed. This didn't surprise him at all. He was invisible not only to most of the students, but to the teachers as well. Most of them took for granted that he'd sit at his desk and do his work without giving them any trouble. He doubted anyone had even noticed he wasn't there.

But that wasn't entirely true. When Nathan returned to his

room to continue working on his robot, he saw that there was a message on his phone from Olivia. *What happened to you today?*

So she'd noticed that he'd gone missing. He sat down on his bed and stared at the message. He wasn't ready to talk to her yet. His thoughts were too jumbled up. Time, that's what he needed.

He forced himself to turn off the phone. He needed all his faculties in working order before he could speak to her, otherwise she'd just re-scramble his thoughts and make everything worse.

Why was being normal so hard? He had his father's golden rules that he always tried his best to follow to the letter but it was like whatever it was inside him that made him different wanted him to fail.

But that wasn't the problem. The problem was Olivia. He couldn't concentrate on his own transformation until hers was complete. And hers was incomplete.

He broke the issue down into smaller pieces, a method he used to identify problems and find solutions.

Number one, Olivia was changing beyond the scope of his control. That point would have to be disregarded. Her behaviour was her doing. He could only offer advice, not affect how she interpreted it.

Number two, he didn't want her to change and this filled him with regret. Another irrelevant point. He could stop helping her, but that wouldn't change actions already in motion.

Number three, her acceptance had happened too smoothly. This fact frustrated him. His intention was for her to be welcomed into the fold, but he'd expected more resistance. This led to the next point.

Number four, he didn't trust Olivia's friends. This was the key problem. A turning point was inevitable.

Nathan had a lot to think about.

12

Olivia was waiting for him before school. He could tell by her folded arms and cross expression that she was angry.

'You didn't reply to my message. What happened yesterday?'

She'd altered her appearance again. The soft downy hairs that clung to her legs were gone. A razor cut on the side of her left knee revealed that she'd started shaving. Her eyelashes were different too. Longer. She was wearing mascara.

'Nathan, I'm talking to you.'

He shook himself free of his sticky daze. 'Sorry, what did you say?'

She rolled her eyes at the sky and grunted. 'Why didn't you reply to my message?'

'Sorry, I had to turn my phone off.'

'But why? That makes no sense.'

He shrugged. 'Now you know how I feel half the time.'

'What? Argh! Never mind. So why did you leave school yesterday?' Her expression softened. 'Was someone mean to you?'

'No. If you must know, my head was a little messed up. And even if someone was mean to me, I can look after myself, okay?'

He started walking past her, and she quickly picked up her bag to follow. 'Do you want to talk about it?'

He looked at the ground. 'No. I'm fine.'

'Okay, okay. I was just worried about you.'

He looked up to see that her face had crumpled. She was hurt by something he'd said. He stopped walking and forced himself to calm down. The last thing he wanted to do was push her away.

'I'm sorry I didn't reply to your message. I will next time,' he said.

'And what makes you so sure there will be a next time?' she said, switching expressions.

He stared at her in bewilderment. 'What do you mean? I thought we were friends.' The words came out louder than he'd intended.

She took a step back and tilted her head in question.

'Sorry. I shouldn't have shouted,' he said. This was a bad start to the day. Very bad.

'It was just a joke,' she said defensively. 'I didn't mean it. It's just something people say to be funny. Never mind.'

He felt the familiar awkwardness return like a closed door between them. 'I have to get to class,' he said. 'Talk to you later.' He walked away quickly before she had a chance to reply.

He'd slipped up by misunderstanding her response, but she kept changing her posture and facial expressions. What was he supposed to do? He decided to employ one of his father's golden rules: he'd pretend that he didn't care. It was a technique he hoped would help change her perception of him. Still, he was worried that he was losing his grip. He would have to work doubly hard to make sure it didn't happen again.

Nathan entered the classroom quickly and sat down at his desk. It was easier for him to view the situation as a mathematical equation. It was the simplest way he knew to predict a likely outcome. Scientists used mathematics to calculate probability all the time. All he needed to do was take himself out of the world for a few minutes. He closed his eyes and waited until the noise of the classroom slowly faded into a nondescript buzz.

First, he needed his parameters. Olivia was one, obviously. As were Virginie, Virginie's friends, school, the number of classes Olivia shared with her new friends, and the time they'd known each other. He also had to take into account tribal behaviour, and past instances in which Virginie and her crew had bullied other students.

He pinched the bridge of his nose. More variables meant more room for error. The problem was becoming too difficult even for him.

His fist slammed into the top of his desk, making everyone around him turn and stare. 'Sorry,' he said to the room at large.

The equation swam around in his mind, but no solution presented itself. He decided that, unlike numbers, people were too complicated. He wished people were more like numbers. He could deal with numbers.

That afternoon Olivia sat on his bed and sketched. She was so absorbed by the task that she didn't even feel the tickle of the ant crawling up her leg. Nathan's fingers twitched to flick it off. Just when he thought he couldn't take it any more, she brushed it away casually.

She was drawing an otter. She was always drawing otters.

'If you're serious about art, you should look at maybe getting a charcoal or graphite pencil. Graphite is good for sketching, like a 6B.'

She looked up. 'What's wrong with my pencil?'

'Nothing. I'm just saying you should maybe look at getting a proper ... Actually, don't worry about it.'

Olivia said nothing and went back to her drawing, using the eraser of her clutch pencil to rub out a bit of the paw she wasn't happy with.

'A 2H is good for fine details like that.'

'Uh huh,' she said without looking up. She was clearly still riled up by their argument that morning. He wished she would say something that consisted of more than two syllables. It was driving him insane.

He leaned forward in his chair, openly staring and watching her every movement. 'Why did you come over if you're not going to talk to me?'

'I am talking to you. I just don't want to discuss stupid pencils,' she replied coolly.

'You're upset. You look upset.'

'I'm not upset.'

'That's such a lie.'

She glared at him and carried on drawing.

He sighed and watched her. 'You draw otters a lot,' he said.

'Yep.'

'One-word answers are a sign of passive aggressiveness. You're doing it on purpose.'

She smiled, and he sank back into his chair and glowered. There was no way they were going to have a normal conversation like this. He swallowed all hope of talking to her about his fears. It was probably best, anyway. He didn't want to spook her.

He stared at her drawing and recalled her story about seeing her first otter with her dad. He sat up. It made so much sense. No wonder she was so obsessed with them. He heard his dad's voice in his mind. *People don't like knowing what's wrong with them, Nathan.*

Olivia probably wasn't even aware of the connection herself. He bit his lip. Telling her would ruin it. She probably wouldn't ever invite him otter-spotting again. He kept quiet.

When she was finished, she held up his drawing for his inspection.

'It's really good,' he said.

'Uh huh. My cheap pencil did that.'

'I didn't mean to criticise you or your pencil.'

'It's fine,' she said, folding up the piece of paper and slipping it inside a notebook.

'You say "fine" like you mean the opposite,' he said.

He watched her replace the book in her satchel. How many pictures were there? He hoped one day to find out.

'I'd better go,' she said, pressing down her skirt with her hands. 'I have to help Ma with dinner tonight.'

'So is that all you came here for? To ignore me?'

She laughed and left without answering.

Mohendra arrived soon after. The two boys went to Nathan's bedroom, where Nathan stood in front of the full-length mirror that hung inside his cupboard door. He didn't think he looked different to anyone else his own age. He was athletically built, thanks to his nightly regime of sit-ups and push-ups before bed.

He didn't enjoy exercise, but he wanted to stay fit to counter all the long hours he spent gaming.

He stood up straighter and pushed his blond hair out of his face. He was too pale, he thought. 'I need a haircut.'

Mohendra groaned from the bed, and Nathan spotted him in the mirror making choking gestures.

Nathan frowned. 'What's wrong with wanting a haircut?'

'It's not the haircut. It's you. You've been going on and on for the past ten minutes. Why do you want to change so much, anyway? It's for this girl, isn't it?'

Nathan continued to study his appearance in the mirror. 'People change to suit their environments all the time. It's all about survival of the fittest.'

'But you hate change. You're like the complete opposite of someone who likes change. Your room has been the same for the last ten years.'

'That's irrelevant. The fact is, I want to change now. None of the guys at school have hair this long.'

Mohendra fell back against the pillows. 'You're worse than a girl. If I close my eyes, it's like I can hear my sister talking.'

'Your sister's voice isn't as deep as mine.'

'Har bloody har.'

Nathan pulled his hair back with his hand to see what it would look like shorter. 'It probably won't make that much difference. People might notice I've changed my hair but will completely lose interest by lunchtime. If they notice at all.'

'That's shocking. Really.'

Nathan ignored Mohendra's comment. 'I wanted to run another idea by you. One of the girls in my class is having a party at the end of the month. I was wondering whether or not I should go.'

'Are you crazy? Did this girl actually invite you to her party? Are you friends with her or any of her friends? Have you ever been to a party? Do you even know what people do at parties?'

'No on all counts.'

'Then why do you want to go?'

'Because Olivia is going.'

Mohendra slapped a hand to his cheek. 'You're being mental.'

Nathan didn't like the idea of gate-crashing Virginie's party either, but he didn't think his classmates would go full *Carrie* on him. He wasn't unpopular. He was just different. 'You could always come with me.'

Mohendra screwed up his face into a look that Nathan had in the past identified as 'dubious' and folded his arms behind his head. 'Well, I don't go to your school, so if it all goes to hell, my reputation won't be tarnished. You can't say the same.'

'I can look after myself.'

'Do you really want to put yourself in a situation like that?'

'If Olivia sees me there, it's one step closer to her accepting me as an equal.'

Mohendra sat up straight. 'Wait. Hang on. This isn't only about impressing Olivia, is it? You still don't trust those girls and you want to make sure nothing happens to her.'

Nathan turned around in surprise. He hadn't thought about that, but now that Mohendra had said it out loud, it made sense.

His thoughtful expression must have given him away because Mohendra laughed and smacked his own leg. 'You are so whipped!'

'Is it so bad to care about someone?'

His serious stare put an end to Mohendra's laughter. 'Okay, I'll go to this stupid party with you. But I'm warning you, if it gets dodgy, we're leaving.'

'Thank you.'

Nathan went back to scrutinising his appearance in the mirror. His jeans were fading, and it was definitely time for new sneakers. 'What do you think I should wear?'

Behind him, Mohendra groaned into his hands.

Nathan got a haircut. Mostly, it went unnoticed, but the experiment did have some unexpected results. One of the jocks in his class, Shaun, shouted, 'Nice do, Langdon,' which Nathan couldn't decide was a compliment or an insult.

The true test came at break, when a giggling procession of teenage girls strode past on their way to the field. From her position at the back, Olivia smiled and passed him a folded-up note before disappearing around the corner.

Nathan unfolded the note in his palm so no passing idiot could swipe it. *I like your hair. You look different.*

He folded the note into his inside blazer pocket and spent the next thirty minutes deciphering her choice of words. By 'different' did she mean 'better'? Was it another sign that she liked him? Passing a note was risky, but it prevented lengthy WhatsApp exchanges that would give the whole game away if one her new friends noticed.

He watched her extra carefully during break. She was still sitting on the outskirts of the group and had yet to penetrate the inner layers of the circle that surrounded Virginie. His mind lingered on that one point. Was it indicative of events to come, he wondered? If Olivia hadn't been accepted into the inner circle, did that mean she wouldn't be accepted at all?

He was being overly paranoid, but he had to be. As much as he tried to teach Olivia to be more observant, she relied on him to be her eyes. It was an impossible situation to be in. He could only trust his instincts and make deductions from what he saw. She had the necessary intel from spending time with the girls. He was operating blindly.

13

Nathan wasn't expecting Olivia to visit him again so soon. He wasn't ready for it either. When she appeared in the doorway of his room, wearing the fake oversized glasses that all the kids at school wore, and that same messy bun that refused to contain her wild black hair, he was filled with a sensation that he was starting to become addicted to. It was a breathless hyper-awareness that made his brain hurt.

He sat up on his bed and closed the Batman comic he'd been reading.

'How's the robot coming?' she asked.

He looked over at the untidy pile of electronic parts and scraps of paper, and wished he'd cleaned up his room. 'It's getting there. My friend Mohendra wants to build one too, so we can make them fight.'

It was unimportant nonsense that she probably wasn't interested in, anyway. It was just a spontaneous project after all, not a hobby.

'You guys are so smart. You'll probably start a software company or something and make millions.'

Olivia threw down her bag and sat down in Nathan's gaming chair. She did an experimental swivel before swinging back to face him.

It was bizarre that she was in his room, in his life, talking about his robot, when a few short weeks ago she was just a girl in his class. But that wasn't entirely true. She'd never been just a girl to him. He was overwhelmed by her, dizzied, like he was falling from a great height.

'Nathan, are you okay?'

'I have to tell you something,' he said.

The force of his words made her rear back slightly and it took a millisecond for her expression to change from soft to serious. 'What is it?'

'I'm worried. I don't trust Virginie and her friends. You need to be very careful around them. I should've told you this before, but I didn't want to hurt your feelings.'

Her eyes widened. 'Why?'

'I just told you why.'

'No, man. Why do I have to be careful?'

He turned away. 'Because they're not nice people. I know it's bad to make assumptions about people without proper data, but I know I'm right about them.'

'Don't be silly. They're normal, just like you and me.'

So she really did think he was normal. Another sign. She never stopped surprising him. But he couldn't think about that. He had to focus.

'Please, Olivia. I'm being serious.'

She laughed. 'So am I. So stop worrying, okay? Everything

is fine. Perfect, even.' She swivelled on the chair and started poking through his electronics with one finger. 'I wish I knew how to make robots. I'd make one to wash the dishes and take out the rubbish bins so I didn't have to.'

He didn't explain that a robot that advanced was way beyond most people's skill, because he didn't think she really wanted to make a robot. People often said things without meaning them. It was one of the reasons he found conversations exhausting.

Just then Wendy pushed open the door with her nose and padded straight to Olivia. She was rewarded with a scratch behind the ear.

'I hated not having friends,' Olivia said, without turning around. 'The loneliness was almost too much. I never understood what was wrong with me, or why it was so hard to make friends with other girls. I had no idea it was all down to tribal behaviour and paying attention. Other people just seemed to get it.' Her voice was as low as a whisper.

Nathan waited for her to speak more, too afraid that anything he said would make her stop.

'I couldn't have done it without you,' she said, without looking up.

He exhaled. He'd been holding his breath. 'But what if they turn on you?' he whispered.

'They won't.'

There was a hardness in her voice that he knew he wouldn't be able to argue with. It was the hardness of hope. She wanted to believe it, and nothing he said was going to change that. So he kept quiet. At least he'd managed to get his feeble warning out. He hoped she'd heard some of it.

Olivia continued to ruffle Wendy's creamy fur and the dog's

tail wagged madly. Nathan got up and pulled the spare office chair that Mohendra usually sat in towards the desk. Olivia watched him work on his robot, occasionally asking questions about what he was doing or why. He liked her company a lot. In the beginning he'd always experienced a panicky feeling that he was losing his mind, but that was slowly going away. It was a different sort of panic now – a panic that she might go away.

When she rested her head on his shoulder, he didn't flinch. But he was acutely aware of her weight, and the tiny bits of hair tickling his neck. He refused to be bothered by it. He concentrated on his work and kept his breathing even. It was hard to focus with her so close, and he was seriously worried that his hands might begin to shake, but she didn't seem to notice.

'Why did you cut your hair?' she asked after what felt like an eternity.

'It was getting too long.'

She nodded into his shoulder. 'I like it. It makes you look like a soccer player or something.'

He laughed. Shorter hair had nothing to do with athletic ability. 'It doesn't make me more aerodynamic or anything.'

He could feel the smile growing on her face, pushing through the material of his T-shirt, penetrating his skin. He held on to the sensation, so that he could remember it and play it back in his mind later. But that was the easy part. He always remembered everything.

That evening Nathan recalled his mom telling him about a distant point of his childhood, a time when as a baby he didn't speak for a long time. He didn't understand why the memory suddenly arose, or what it meant, but once open, he found himself musing on it.

In crèche all the other babies had already mastered 'Mama' and 'Dada' and 'want', but not Nathan. He smiled and laughed just like all the others, but no words ever left his lips. It was around that time that the paediatricians started diagnosing several different conditions, before eventually settling on autism spectrum disorder, or ASD. Nathan was yanked from crèche and deposited in a school for special children where he was given plastic blocks to play with while a woman with a mustard-coloured file watched what he did.

Nathan eventually learned how to speak and began driving his parents crazy by repeating random words over and over again, regardless of whether they were at home or in the shops. His mom told the story like it was a fond memory, but he remembered the time she'd told one of her friends that she regretted having had a baby.

What Nathan's mother didn't realise, or perhaps didn't choose to see, was that Nathan had what the doctors called perfect recall: he could remember every tiny detail, including that time in his childhood when his mother wished he hadn't been born, and every time since then that she'd repeated the sentiment.

14

It was still light enough to walk to the party from Mohendra's place. While the Chettys lived in a big house, it was nothing compared to Virginie's parents' estate in the leafy upper-class part of Wynberg. Nathan and Mohendra passed several large homes obscured by security fencing, and long tree-lined avenues that got bigger the further they walked. Huge muscular dobermanns watched them pass.

'Why are we doing this?' asked Mohendra.

'Is that a real question?'

Mohendra rolled his eyes. 'No. I just have a bad feeling, that's all.'

Mohendra's parents were wealthy, and had no problem buying him an entire seasonal wardrobe of new clothes. His cupboard boasted all name-brand tags. Nathan had borrowed a few items for the party, including a pair of Levi 501 jeans, and a T-shirt from a boutique in Kloof Street. Mohendra had insisted that Nathan wear the gear if he wanted to make a good impression.

'I just hope none of the jocks try to steal the clothes off your back. My mom will kill me.'

Nathan frowned. He knew that if he got into an altercation he wasn't supposed to show any signs of weakness or fear, but he didn't want to put his friend in danger. 'Do you think they'll try and make trouble with us?' For a brief second, he considered turning back.

'I don't know. Maybe. They're jocks, right? You know them better than I do.'

'That's the problem, I do.'

'Why have we stopped walking?' Mohendra asked.

Nathan stood on the pavement. A car full of young people sped past, their screams and wolf whistles echoing in the otherwise quiet street. 'If you don't want to go, then let's turn around and go back,' he said.

Mohendra kicked an empty cooldrink can with the tip of his sneaker. 'I said I'd go with you, and we've come this far. If we turn back now, we'll just be losers.'

'Alright. I'm cool. Are you cool?'

'I'm cool.'

They were both nervous, but Nathan knew if one backed down, the other would follow. They had to go on.

Mohendra checked the leaked invite on his phone. 'This is the place,' he said, glancing up at the massive gates.

There was a single pink balloon hanging from the tall black wrought-iron gates outside Virginie's house. Someone had burst the others, and all that remained of them were a couple of pink plastic tatters on the ground.

They walked up the long winding driveway lined with tall oak trees, their feet scrunching on the pebbles. A squirrel darted up a trunk as they passed. The property was so big that if they hadn't known better, they could easily have mistaken it for a park. As they rounded a bend, the vast outline of the white house became visible. It was a double-storey mansion, with large slatted windows and creepers running up the right side.

'Is Virginie single?' asked Mohendra.

Nathan shrugged. 'I have no idea. I can ask Olivia if you want?'

'Please don't. It was a joke.'

The sound of high-pitched laughter was coming from another path that veered between the trees.

'Do you think we should go down there?' asked Mohendra.

More screaming and laughing pierced the air. Nathan's palms began to sweat and a prickly feeling blossomed at the base of his neck. He forced his feet to move, one step at a time. Mohendra was being uncharacteristically unsure of himself as well.

The voices grew louder the further they walked down the wooded path, and soon they found evidence of the party underway – a beer can tossed into a bush, and a crushed cigarette, still smoking. The path ended, revealing a snapshot of something neither of them had ever seen before – a teen party in all its glory.

At the centre was a poolhouse, its doors and floor-to-ceiling windows thrown open. There were teenagers everywhere – standing in small groups, jumping on the protective pool covering as if it were a trampoline, causing water to spill over the sides, and standing around a fire that wasn't being tended by anyone.

As Nathan and Mohendra took it all in, music began to blast from inside the poolhouse – Steve Aoki or Haezer or one of the popular DJs of the moment, Nathan couldn't make out which above the distortion of the speakers. He didn't understand how anyone could enjoy music that loud. You couldn't appreciate it.

'Well, we're here,' said Mohendra, rubbing his hands together and acting more like himself. 'Might as well get this over with.'

'What? Okay.'

Nathan walked forward purposefully and recognised a lot of faces from school. He hadn't realised that so many of them were going to be at the party, a stupid oversight on his part. He felt afraid. He hated crowds. It had taken him ages to get comfortable with the school setting, and he certainly wasn't cut out for parties.

Any minute now he was going to forget how to breathe and it would be all over. Panic reared up inside him, reminding him of its presence. He wanted to go home.

Shaun did a double-take when he spotted Nathan approaching. 'Hey, it's Langdon. Cool threads, my man.'

'Hey, Shaun.' His mouth was dry.

'You want a beer, dude? What about your buddy?'

'Sure,' answered Mohendra, before Nathan had a chance to refuse.

Shaun tossed them each a can. 'It's so cool to see you here, dude. Just grab another beer if you want one.'

'Thanks,' replied Nathan, who had no intention of doing so.

Shaun wandered off to speak to someone else and Mohendra cracked open his can and took a sip. 'Maybe I was wrong about this lot,' he said with a grimace.

'It could have gone either way. You had no way of knowing whether they were going to accept us or not,' replied Nathan.

'Dude, seriously. Try to keep the robot talk to a minimum, okay? We're in public.'

They headed in the direction of a fallen log and took a seat. More guys from Nathan's class greeted them. There were several more offers of beer. More kids from school arrived, mostly girls.

A large percentage of the party had squeezed themselves into the poolhouse. Nathan could make out dancing figures through the windows. There was no sign of Olivia or her friends. Faces, some familiar and others not, came and went, and ran into each other and hugged and laughed. It was loud and wild, and Nathan felt more uncomfortable than ever. The noise and activity were disorienting and only fed his panic.

Mohendra, on the other hand, was bouncing his leg in time to the music, clearly eager to dance. Nathan was grateful to have his friend with him. He wouldn't have been able to come alone.

The sky was darkening, and one of the school jocks decided to squirt something flammable into the fire, which raged and sparked at everyone around it. The music and the laughter grew louder.

Mohendra took Nathan's unopened beer and drank it.

As thirsty as he was, Nathan had no interest in drinking alcohol. Not for the first time, he wished he was at home, at his desk. He felt completely out of place, like an alien that didn't understand a thing about the planet it had just landed on.

Two guys holding each other around the shoulders stumbled over. 'Langdon!' shouted the one on the left. His name was Craig, and he was a rugby jock.

'Hey, Craig.'

'Oh man, Langdon's here,' Craig told his companion gleefully.

'Hey, Langdon!' echoed the friend.

Nathan wasn't sure whether he was being mocked or not.

'This is my brother, Chris. He was expelled. Man, how cool is that?' Craig pulled his brother into a headlock and rubbed his fist vigorously on his head.

Mohendra leaned closer to Nathan. 'Those guys are wasted,' he whispered.

The tussle escalated into a pushing match. Nathan leaned out of the way. Beside him, Mohendra watched with interest, the fire reflecting in his eyes.

The brothers stopped pushing and glared at each other. They puffed themselves up to try and intimidate each other, but the posturing didn't last and they burst out laughing. Nathan recognised this as typical jock behaviour.

Craig replaced his arm around his brother's shoulder. 'Langdon is the class's genius.'

'Oh ja? Hey, Langdon, what's eighty-five times ninety?'

'Seven thousand six hundred and fifty.'

Both brothers stared at Nathan in open-mouthed surprise. 'Woah.'

As Nathan and Mohendra sat on their log in the shadow of the sputtering fire, they were joined by even more guys from the class. Mohendra accepted another beer.

'You're cool, Langdon,' said Shaun, who'd just pitched up, complaining that he'd lost his shoes.

Nathan nodded. He hadn't done anything noteworthy to earn the compliment. He'd just showed up.

The guys were happy to joke among themselves, without his active involvement. Mohendra was having a great time, laughing and drinking. Nathan could tell by the colour in his friend's cheeks that he was getting drunk. He would have to intervene if Mohendra drank any more.

He kept looking around and finally spotted a dark head in the crowd. The rest of the party disappeared. She was wearing a blue vest over denim shorts. He could see the strings of her red bikini top peeking out at the shoulders. She had stripy sandals on, with long bows wrapped around her ankles.

She hadn't spotted him. She was too busy laughing with her friends.

A hard rap on his arm jolted him back to reality.

'What do you think, Langdon? Isn't that hilarious?'

Nathan had no idea what they were talking about. Mohendra nodded vigorously in his direction. 'Very funny,' he said, putting on his best fake smile.

'See? I told you he had a sense of humour.' Shaun turned to Nathan, subjecting him to a sweaty arm around his neck. 'I told them,' he said, swaying.

The utter ridiculousness of the situation made Nathan burst out laughing. This satisfied the rest of the group, who started debating which members of the faculty were secretly dating each other. Craig and his brother Chris wandered off in the direction of the poolhouse.

Nathan pried Shaun's arm off his shoulder and pulled Mohendra aside. 'I'm going to go find Olivia. Are you going to stay here?'

'Ja. These guys are awesome. Good luck, man.'

Nathan felt guilty about leaving Mohendra behind, but he needed to get to Olivia. He pushed his way through an impossible number of bodies. He was invisible again, just the way he liked it.

So many of his classmates were drunk. The ground was muddy from spilled alcohol and pool water churned up by stomping feet. He searched above the heads for Olivia but she'd disappeared again.

'Hello, Nathan.'

He spun on the spot and found himself face to face with Virginie. He froze, just like when he and Mohendra used to play Red Light, Green Light as children. She was alone, which only made her more intimidating. Her blonde hair was pulled up into a tight bun on top of her head, and her eyes were made up dramatically with glittery black eyeshadow.

'Hi.' He couldn't think of anything else to say to her. She'd never spoken to him before.

Virginie stared at him lazily from her casual position against the wall. 'I don't remember inviting you,' she said.

He shrugged. The truth was that everyone was sharing the invite on WhatsApp, but he didn't want to argue with Virginie in case she had him thrown out.

'You're friends with Olivia, aren't you?'

He stared at her. The revelation that she knew private details of his life unnerved him. He'd given absolutely no thought to the idea that the girls he'd been studying, had been studying him too. Why would Virginie even care about him or who he hung out with?

'Yes, we're friends,' he replied carefully.

Suddenly she didn't look so bored any more. She straightened up in one catlike motion, and a smirk began to grow at the corners of her mouth. He braced himself.

'If you're looking for her, I saw her go behind the poolhouse,' she said silkily, running her fingers across his arm as she circled him. It felt like claws on his bare skin. Her voice sounded deceptively sweet.

He didn't thank her, but walked resolutely towards the far end of the poolhouse.

Nathan didn't trust Virginie. He knew he wasn't wrong about her. Either she was leading him in the wrong direction or she was trying to trick him in some other way.

He turned the corner and started walking towards the back of the building. It was darker here, and the music was muffled. Nathan slowed his steps. If someone was waiting for him, he didn't want to be too easy a target. There were plenty of trees to hide behind. Keeping one hand on the wall, he moved forward carefully.

There were voices up ahead. Laughter. A ball of ice was developing in his stomach. What was Virginie planning? It was possible he'd underestimated her intelligence. If that was the case, then she was even more dangerous than he'd thought.

Instead of peeking around the corner, he veered left and concealed himself behind a tree. When he was sure no one had seen him, he risked peering out from behind the trunk. He could just make out the tall figure of Craig's brother, Chris, staggering around in the darkness. He leaned his head out more to try and see more clearly. Chris was with someone. A girl.

The ball of ice exploded along with Nathan's thoughts, piercing him with the shards. *Please don't be Olivia. Please don't be Olivia. Please don't be Olivia.*

The pair stumbled towards him. They were lip-locked to each other, staggering around and laughing. Drunk. Nathan watched as they lowered themselves to the ground. He stared, silently wishing, repeating the words *not Olivia* in his head.

Then the girl turned around. He could clearly make out her dark skin, her black hair falling out of its bun. Her eyes were closed, her lips slightly parted. Craig pulled at the red bikini straps on her shoulders.

Nathan stepped forward to intervene, when Olivia's high-pitched laughter filled the air. They were both laughing.

She was allowing him to do it.

Nathan didn't stay a second longer but marched back the way he'd come, not caring if she saw him or if the loud crunch of his footsteps gave him away. He needed to get as far away from the party as possible.

He pulled his phone out of his pocket and messaged Mohendra to say he was leaving, and to meet him in the road.

Faces became unrecognisable around him. None of it mattered. The coldness took over his entire body. It seeped into his brain, freezing the thoughts that hung there, keeping them in stasis. He needed to get away.

She's not for you. That's what he told himself as he sat on the pavement outside the estate. *She's not for you.*

He wished the coldness would numb his heart and freeze his brain so he didn't have to deal with what he'd just seen.

15

When Nathan arrived home, his parents were waiting for him in the lounge. They didn't look angry. He looked up at the wall clock. It was only just past nine.

'Why are you staring at me like that?' he asked.

His parents glanced at each other. His dad wiped his hand over his face. 'Mohendra's mother called. She said Mohendra came home drunk. She's very angry.'

'That's putting it mildly,' added his mother.

His dad gave her a sharp look and returned his attention to his son. 'Can you tell us what happened? Where were you?'

Nathan shrugged. 'We went to a party and he drank too much. I don't understand why you're angry. I didn't drink and I'm home early.' He couldn't have this conversation with them. He needed to be alone.

'We're not angry,' said his mom.

'You look angry.'

'Mrs Chetty says you took Mohendra to the party,' his dad said. 'Is that true?'

'Yes. So what?'

'Since when do you go to parties?' his mother asked.

'What's wrong with me going to a party?'

'And there was alcohol at this party?'

'Obviously.' Couldn't they see that he really didn't want to talk?

His mother opened her mouth to speak again but his dad held up a hand to stop her. 'Why don't you go to bed so long, while your mother and I talk for a little while? I'll be with you shortly.'

'Okay.'

Nathan went through the motions of brushing his teeth and changing into his pyjamas. The icy feeling was still there. It deepened with every second that passed.

He got under the covers and lay on his back. His mind went back to the party and he replayed the image of Olivia and Chris kissing, and their tangle of limbs, the snap of her bikini strap. He'd been stupid to think that she liked him in the same way that he liked her. They were just friends, and he was just Nathan, the weirdo in class. The signs that he thought he'd seen were all in his head.

He heard his door open and his dad came in. Nathan continued to stare at the ceiling.

'Hey, kiddo. How're you doing?'

The pressure on the bed told him his dad had sat down.

'I still don't know what I did wrong.'

His father sighed. 'We're just trying to figure out what happened. Why didn't you try to stop Mohendra when he started drinking too much?'

'I wasn't with him the whole time.' The words were thick in his mouth.

'Ah. Was Olivia there?'

Nathan's eyes felt heavy. There was a sadness lurking there, threatening to spill out. No matter how he looked at it, there could only be one conclusion.

'I don't think you guys need to worry about Olivia any more.'

'Why? What happened?'

Nathan's pressed his lips together to keep the words inside.

His dad put a hand on his knee. 'You really liked that girl, didn't you?'

All Nathan could do was nod.

'It happens to us all. I had my heart broken a few times when I was your age.'

Nathan turned to the wall, his eyes burning.

'You're a good kid, Nathan. Always remember that. One day you're going to make a great boyfriend to some lucky girl.'

'Then why doesn't she think so?'

His father hesitated. 'I don't know. You haven't really told me anything about this girl. Do you want to talk about it?'

Nathan shook his head.

'Okay, Nathan. But I'm here if you ever want to.'

His father switched off the light before he left, something he hadn't done in years, but the darkness didn't stop the images from flashing in Nathan's mind. Olivia and Chris staggering around, their mouths sucking at each other's faces like fish while the music thundered in the background. He pressed his eyelids closed and concentrated on the image. He didn't want to love her. Not if she didn't love him back.

The thought of Olivia leading Chris down to the muddy

banks of the Liesbeek River to look for otters caused a jolt of pain in his chest. He couldn't imagine that. He had to stop. It was too painful.

Nathan's father decided to take him out on Saturday. Nathan appreciated the gesture: he needed some space away from his room, and a distraction from the constant replay he'd been torturing himself with.

They went to the driving range. Nathan suspected his father might have needed some time out of the house too.

He sat on a bench while his dad shunted balls towards a distant target. There were only a few other people at the range. Most seemed to be aiming at a workman driving a yellow lawn-mower across the grass. Nathan watched the progress of the balls rise and fall on the bright-green grass. The morning sky was pale blue, with shades of white lining the horizon.

His thoughts drifted to Olivia. He wondered if she'd got home alright, if she was safe at home, or if she'd drunk too much and was suffering with an unfamiliar hangover.

'Loving someone is one of the most difficult things you'll experience. It's extra hard when your love isn't reciprocated. You can't turn those feelings off. And most of the time there's nothing you can do to change that person's mind.'

Nathan listened to his father's words without taking his eyes off the field. When he didn't respond, his father leaned on his driver.

'How're you doing?'

Nathan looked up. How could he explain to his father what he was feeling? The truth was, he felt hollow. There was a giant emptiness in him. His life had always been so routine. He'd lived with the comfort that no surprises were waiting to derail his existence. He was always careful, always cautious. Olivia had offered a different, unknown path. Nathan had wanted to know what might happen between them. He was excited at the prospect. But that was all gone and he was lost. There was nothing but the awareness of unfulfilled happiness.

He inhaled deeply before answering. 'I don't know, Dad. I'm pretty sad.'

His father nodded, then grinned. 'Remember what I told you before. Pretend you don't care. Play it cool. It will drive her crazy.'

Nathan nodded. Mohendra had offered the same advice. His exact words were that girls hated not getting attention, especially when they were used to it. He'd tried to play it cool when he was pretending to be normal, but that was different. He hadn't been trying to hide a broken heart.

'Will it work?'

His father laughed. 'Of course it will. It's called playing the game, kiddo. It's part of life.'

Nathan sighed. He wished life could go back to the way it was before he'd started having feelings for Olivia. Life was simpler then.

His father's body relaxed. Clearly, he'd said what he wanted to say. He turned back to his game, and launched a ball with a little more vigour than before.

Nathan leaned back against the wall. What if Olivia had used him to become popular? What if she was only pretending to be his friend in the same way that she was pretending to fit in with Virginie and her friends?

The thought made him feel sick. He knew he was different from everyone else, but he never for one second thought of himself as naive. He tried so hard not to be. But worse than that, he felt like a fool.

16

Olivia didn't contact him the entire weekend, nor did he try and contact her. The first time Nathan saw her was the following week, in biology class. He didn't greet her when he passed her desk but walked straight to his own.

Shaun stood and raised his hand for a high five. 'Langdon!' he said, with exaggerated excitement.

Nathan smacked his hand against Shaun's before sitting down, even though he didn't have any hand sanitiser on him. He concentrated on not touching his face with that hand so that he didn't transfer any germs.

Olivia had turned around in her seat and stared at the exchange with obvious wide-eyed surprise. Nathan purposely didn't meet her gaze, but resolutely removed his books from his bag. He was too hurt to look at her.

He spent the entire morning in a state of hyper-awareness. His invisibility shield was gone, leaving him vulnerable and open. It was like standing on a high ledge, with no safety net underneath. Each time he walked into a class, he wasn't sure what to expect. It was only towards lunchtime that he realised that the guys greeting him and slapping him on the back weren't teasing him. He started to relax, although the bitter disappointment he felt about Olivia still dominated his thoughts and his mood.

She tried to speak to him when the lunch bell rang. 'Why didn't you tell me you were going to the party, Nathan?'

He walked straight past her. He had no intention of answering her, even though it felt like little stabs in his heart every time he ignored her.

'Nathan?'

He could feel her watching him as he walked away.

For the first time in a long time, Nathan didn't eat his lunch under his tree. Instead, he found an empty table in the noisy cafeteria. He didn't want to see Olivia. He didn't what to hear her laugh or see her smile. He wanted that short period when they were friends, or pretending to be friends, to disappear.

His sandwich tasted bland and stale. He was eating more out of necessity than enjoyment. But as much as he wanted to keep his thoughts free of her, his memories kept playing back in his brain without mercy. By the time lunch ended, he felt like he'd been smashed into the floor by his emotions. He wanted to talk to her. He never wanted to talk to her again. The two thoughts vied with each other like two evenly matched Mortal Kombat fighters.

Knowing that Olivia was in his next class, he kept his eyes down as he walked to his desk and quickly unpacked his books. Nathan could feel her gaze on him, but he refused to look up. He opened his textbook as he sat down, and hid behind it.

Their homework had been to answer a series of questions

about a passage from Shakespeare's *Othello*. Nathan's pencil moved mechanically across his answers. He hadn't given much thought to the assignment, so he wasn't surprised when most of his answers turned out to be wrong. His pencil rapped against the desk. His concentration was slipping fast. Mrs Booysen's voice sounded ten kilometres away. He felt trapped in his own head again.

When a note was passed to his desk, he felt like the writing on it was burning into his corneas. Nathan grabbed it quickly, and crumpled it up in his fist. He didn't want any form of communication with her and wished she would just stop trying. He didn't want her handwriting to imbed itself in his brain.

He didn't meet her gaze when he left class, but he heard her school shoes slapping against the tiled hallway as she ran after him. 'Nathan. Wait!'

If he carried on walking, he hoped she'd think he hadn't heard her. The corridors were always noisy when the bell rang – people all shouting at once as they rushed past, with hollow laughter echoing off the red-brick walls.

He'd made it out the school's front door when she gripped him by the shoulder and swung him around.

'What is your problem?' she yelled, her cheeks red from running. Her hair had unravelled, and loose pieces were escaping everywhere.

A hundred different sentences wrestled on his tongue. He wanted to ask her to explain why she'd used him. He wanted to tell her to go away and leave him alone forever. But mostly he wanted her to tell him that what had happened on Friday night between her and Chris had been a huge mistake. But he didn't say any of those things.

'I can't talk to you,' he said, turning to walk away.

'Why? What's happened? Nathan!'

He made it as far as the school gates this time, before she caught up to him. Other students were openly staring.

'Leave me alone, Olivia.'

'No!' She darted in front of him to block his way. 'What's going on? Why won't you talk to me?'

He looked away so he didn't have to meet her gaze. 'Get out the way,' he said.

'Why are you acting so weird?' She was shouting and shifting from side to side to try and get in front of him, determined to meet his gaze.

He pushed past her to get as far away as possible from the small crowd that was forming around them.

'Nathan!'

At home, he retreated to his room, slamming the door behind him.

His mother had been in to clean, despite the fact that she knew he didn't like anyone touching his stuff. He balled up his fists. Why were the women in his life so infuriating?

His backpack landed on the floor with a thud. Nathan uncurled his fingers and made straight for his desk to rearrange everything as it had been before. The stationery holder was on the right-hand side, his desk lamp on the left. It was obviously symmetrical. How could she not see that? How could she not remember to put things back the way they were after moving them?

He replaced the Han Solo Lego mini figure in its proper spot with trembling fingers. He hadn't been so upset in a long time. He needed something to take his mind off things.

He'd just powered on his laptop to play a game when Olivia appeared in the doorway, clutching the strap of her bag, her eyes red.

Nathan glanced at her. Was she crying for real or pretending? He drew his fingers through his hair. 'Why won't you just leave me alone?'

Olivia chewed on her bottom lip. 'I don't understand why you're angry with me.' She took a step into the room and hesitated. 'What happened to make you hate me so much?'

He stared at the ceiling. He hated her for invading his personal space. His room was his escape from the rest of the world. It shouldn't be that easy for someone to walk in and disturb his peace, especially someone he wanted to avoid.

'I don't have anything to say to you, Olivia. Go home.'

She took a sharp breath, but remained where she was. 'Did someone say something to you? At the party?'

He didn't speak, but rather hoped the silence would convey what was on his mind.

'I know you were there. Mandy told me she saw you. And I saw how all the guys were carrying on with you this morning. So tell me, what happened at the party that you aren't telling me?'

He stared at her shoes, willing her to read the truth from his mind. But before he could say anything, her lips parted and a string of words came out, her voice rising higher and higher the more she wound herself up. 'I don't remember anything from the party. I was drunk, and before you start judging me, it was the first time I've ever got so drunk. And they made me drink too much on purpose. I was puking everywhere. I can't even remember how I got home. So if that's it, then I'm sorry, but I really don't remember.'

'It's not that,' he said. 'I saw you making out with Chris behind the poolhouse.'

Her mouth opened for another outburst when her eyes widened in recollection. 'Oh.'

For some weird reason, Olivia knowing what was wrong made him feel worse. Shame hit him like a slap in the face, and he swivelled towards his screen so that she couldn't see the colour in his cheeks – but not before noticing that she'd flushed too.

She stood in the doorway for what felt like an eternity, while they purposely looked everywhere but at each other. He wanted her to leave, but his voice was trapped in the chaos of his thoughts. He wished an asteroid would crash through the roof and end his misery so he didn't have to deal with the situation.

'Do you even like him?' The words were out of his mouth before he could stop them. He closed his eyes, wishing he could take them back.

Olivia started spluttering. 'I don't … What does it even matter?'

Out the corner of his eye he saw her readjust her bag on her shoulder and take a step back, knocking one of his action figures to the floor. 'I'm sorry,' she said, before disappearing out the door.

Nathan stared at his screen, waiting for the front door to slam.

It was hours before his heart stopped beating at breakneck speed.

With Mohendra grounded, Nathan felt truly alone. This was a most distressing frame of mind to be in and it was impossible to distract himself from his own thoughts.

He logged on to Facebook but Mohendra wasn't online. He tried the Discord channel they both belonged to but Mohendra wasn't there either.

Usually he could spend hours chatting to other online gamers but it was always trivial stuff that didn't matter – the changing nature of time in the comic-book universe and how that always screwed up storylines, and which community members were suspected to be part of Anonymous and why – a topic that always made him laugh.

To them he was G_Nat. They didn't know anything about his life. But more than that, they didn't care, just like he didn't care about them. They were okay company when he was gaming, but now that he actually needed to talk to someone, they were as useful as the action figures on his desk.

Nathan leaned across and hit the power button, preferring instead to stare at the wall until a better alternative presented itself. He didn't want to continue working on his robot, and he didn't want to read either. Everything frustrated him and nothing could make him feel better.

His mother came in, carrying fresh laundry, and switched on the light. She yelped when she saw him sitting at the desk and dropped the clothes on the floor.

'Nathan, why are you sitting in the dark?'

He shrugged and continued to stare at the wall. It was a bit more interesting now that he could actually see it.

She tutted loudly and bent down to pick up the laundry.

'Come to the lounge. We can watch something on Netflix if you want.'

'No thanks.'

'Nathan, sweetheart, you can't just sit in the dark.'

'Why not?'

'Because ... Well, I'm sure it's not good for your eyes.'

He didn't want to argue. He had no energy for it, or for anything else.

She dumped the rescued clothing on his bed. 'Mohendra won't be grounded forever. He'll be back before you know it.'

Nathan turned around in irritation. 'But I need to speak to him now and he never replies to his WhatsApp messages.'

His mother stood for a moment and stared into space. 'Look, I really wish I could help, Nathan. I really do. Why don't you keep trying to get hold of him? He has to respond eventually.'

When she'd left, Nathan turned his attention back to the wall. There was no point messaging Mohendra and waiting for his reply. He needed a sounding board now. His mind was a labyrinth of thoughts running in a hundred different directions. He needed to push away the pain and focus on a way to get past this.

The wall disappeared as Nathan's thoughts spun round and round. His attempt to change himself had backfired badly. He knew that to save himself any more heartache, he'd have to go back to the beginning, to the way things were before he tried to help Olivia. It would have to be like the past few weeks had never happened.

17

Nathan fell back into his old routine. His phone alarm was set for six every morning. When he woke, he sat on the floor with his feet tucked underneath his bed and did fifty sit-ups, followed by a breakfast of Jungle Oats with hot water and honey. At six-thirty-five he washed his face and brushed his teeth, dressed and said goodbye to Wendy before leaving the house.

His school day was divided into forty-five-minute segments interspersed with two half-hour breaks. It helped to compartmentalise his time like this, to break it down into numbers that he could rely on.

There were fourteen steps on the staircase leading from the first floor to the second, but only thirteen stairs leading from the second to the third. There were thirty-three paces between his English class and history, three hundred and sixty-five pages in his history textbook, seven pencils stuck into the ceiling panels in the biology class, a hundred and two segments in the body of the earthworm they were studying, one hundred and ninety-eight words in the school song the students sang at the end of the day.

The numbers helped him to avoid thinking about Olivia. He knew he looked like an idiot every time he passed her, his lips moving quickly as he counted under his breath, but it got him through the day.

Still, for all these efforts, Nathan felt heavy with the knowledge that his life had changed. No matter how much he tried to turn back the hours, his existence had shifted to a different plane. Olivia had changed him as much as he had helped her change herself. He couldn't rewind or erase what had happened.

By the time he got home after school, he was miserable again, his bag heavy, his uniform constricting. For the first time in a very long time, he didn't know what to do.

He needed to speak to the one person he had left. Mohendra.

'I'm not grounded any more. My parents battled it out and decided that I'm allowed to make some mistakes. Ha! I was lucky.'

Sitting on his bed, listening to his best friend talk himself in circles, Nathan remembered how Mrs Chetty had called his parents, acting like it was all his fault. 'You know what? Please don't ever blame me again to get yourself out of trouble.'

Mohendra scoffed and waved his hand dismissively. 'Your parents are cool. It's mine that are the problem. I'm sorry about the call, man, but you know how my mom gets when she's worked up.'

Nathan said nothing. It was a lame excuse. Just meaningless words.

'And don't even worry about Olivia. You know how fickle girls are.'

Nathan understood that Mohendra existed on the basis that everybody else was to blame for his misfortunes, and was trying to convince Nathan to adopt the same thinking. He was animated in his argument, throwing his hands around in the air as he spoke.

Nathan listened quietly without interrupting. The feeling of ice in his veins was back. Even Mohendra's peace offering of McDonald's burgers didn't make him feel better.

'Dude, it's your first broken heart. It's better that it happened now, so that it's not so bad the next time. Trust me.'

Nathan felt the heat grow in his cheeks. Talking to Mohendra could sometimes be impossible. 'How would you know?' he asked. 'And anyway, I did nothing wrong. I didn't need your mom dumping on me after what happened with Olivia.'

'Olivia. Olivia. Olivia. Dude, you're not the one who was grounded.'

'You were ungrounded!'

'Why are you shouting?'

'Because you're not seeing my point and you're being selfish!'

Mohendra grabbed his laptop and shoved it into his backpack and zipped it closed. He stood, his expression hard and angry. 'And you always think your point is the only one that counts.'

'Where are you going?' asked Nathan.

'Home.'

Nathan didn't stop him from leaving, but once the front door had slammed, he grabbed a jersey and headed out the back door.

He was shaking with anger. He and Mohendra had never fought before. Worse, the fight had been about nothing. Why had he lashed out like that? Everything he valued was slipping out of his grip.

For the second time, he felt the need to get away from his life. The fundamental flaw of this reasoning, however, was that wherever he went, his thoughts would follow.

Nathan let his feet carry him down one street after another, careful to avoid a route that would cross with Mohendra's. After ten minutes of walking, he found himself in the older part of Rosebank, where the pavements were solid granite and the original cobblestones peeked out through the tar. The quiet was getting to him, so he inserted his earbuds and blasted music to stop his mind repeating his argument with Mohendra, or, worse, his last exchange with Olivia.

Increasing his pace in time to the beat, he concentrated on the ancient wrought-iron gates of old homes and the tall spires of the mansions that hid among the gnarled trees. He hardly ever came to this side of the neighbourhood. The unfamiliarity was strangely soothing. His meander led him to the entrance of a park where people could let their dogs run free among the trees.

He stopped short. His feet had taken him right up to the Liesbeek Canal, which ran all the way to the river. It was like someone had hit the 'play' button in his brain. Vivid recollections of that cold muddy morning on the bank searching for otters invaded his mind.

Nathan closed his eyes and pinched the bridge of his nose with his fingers. He was in so much pain. All he'd done was open himself up to another person. *How did it go so wrong?*

He increased the volume of the music and turned his back on the canal. But he realised he had nowhere to go except back home. Turning around again, he sat down on the edge of the canal and let his legs dangle over the side. The water here was only a trickle, but it was as brown as the river had been that morning. There were seventeen patches of grass between the cracks on the canal floor, fifty-two cracks, three plastic bags.

He wondered if the Cape clawless otter ever ventured as far as the canal. And just like that, Olivia was back in his thoughts. He wondered if her new life as one of the school A-listers meant that she'd left her love of otters behind. As he studied the muddy water, it struck him that Olivia was similar in nature to the creatures she loved – elusive and wild. If he got too close, he would get bitten. And now that he'd been bitten, he never wanted to feel that pain again.

Thirty-three ants walked in a straight line beneath his feet.

Shut up. Shut up. Shut up. Shut up.

18

Nathan searched the school for a new lunch-break spot, one that would afford him privacy and quiet. The solution was a cement step facing a small avenue of trees leading to the netball court. It was just as peaceful as his last spot, with less foot traffic, and it meant he never had to see Olivia. Most of the students spent break on the soccer field.

His father had made him a sandwich that morning. He could tell because it was inexpertly wrapped in clingwrap, which was bunched up at the bottom. Nathan peeled apart his bread to see what was on it. Cheese and apricot jam. He took a bite. It wasn't awful. And his dad had used too much butter, which somehow reminded him of Christmas leftover sandwiches.

What he liked about this new position was that the birds twittered from the trees, so if he closed his eyes, he could be in a forest somewhere far away. It helped him forget where he was. But it didn't make him happy. No amount of imagining could.

In class, Shaun leaned across his desk and prodded Nathan on the shoulder. 'Hey, Langdon. What's up with you and Olivia? You used to be so tight and now, well ...'

Nathan stiffened. Shaun had never spoken to him in class before. He looked up from his notebook. 'Me and Olivia?'

'Is it because of ... you know?'

'Because of what?'

Shaun looked around to make sure no one was listening in on their conversation and lowered his voice. 'Because she hooked up with Chris at the party? I know how you feel. I can't tell you how many times a girl has done that to me.'

Nathan wished he could go back to being invisible. How could Shaun expect him to discuss something so private when they weren't even friends? And, besides that, Nathan didn't know what Shaun's motivation was for talking to him. It could be a trick.

When Nathan didn't respond, Shaun continued, 'Ag, bru, you'll be alright. There are loads of other girls out there. Just you wait. And don't even worry about her. You're better off. She's got a bit of a reputation, if you know what I mean.'

Nathan tilted his head to show that he was listening.

'One of the girls told me. Said Olivia went to watch Craig play a league match and spent the whole night flirting with the rival team's defender. Said Olivia didn't even bat an eyelid when Craig dumped her. You can't trust girls, hey?'

Nathan didn't speak. He hoped that Shaun would take the hint and go away. He recognised false news when he heard it. He didn't believe Olivia was capable of doing what Shaun had described. He resisted the urge to defend her, reminding himself that she wasn't his problem any more.

But Shaun wasn't going to be deterred that easily. 'There's a party at the community hall this weekend, with club DJs and everything. I'm sure you'll meet loads of girls there. You must bring your Muslim friend with. He's a laugh, that one.'

'He's Indian,' corrected Nathan automatically.

'Ja, him.'

There was nowhere Nathan wanted to be less, but that wasn't Shaun's business. He picked up his textbook resolutely, hoping this time Shaun would finally take the hint. Shaun settled back behind his desk, but his words remained.

As much as he tried not to look at her, Nathan couldn't help notice that Olivia had transformed again. Her hair was lighter. She'd applied some treatment to it, but there was no blonde underneath her natural black to prevent the harsh shade of orange that shone through the carefully applied hairpins. Her skin was also different, like the make-up she wore had lightened her natural tone.

The new transformation had resulted in a fraying around the edges – her nerviness was back, as was her telltale low confidence that showed itself in the way she wrung her hands or bit her lip when she thought no one was looking. Whenever one of the girls spoke to her, the new Olivia would spring back into the right shape. She marched behind them in perfect step, one foot in front of the other, in time with theirs. Yet while they retained their perfect smiles, Olivia did not.

Had she heard the rumours about her, he wondered?

Nathan forced himself to look away. After everything that had happened between them, he couldn't exactly go up to her and give her advice on how to carry herself. That part of their lives was over. She was on her own now.

She looked at him as she passed. He'd always been so careful to avoid other people's gazes, but he was incapable of stopping himself from looking into her brown eyes. It was only for a moment, but it was clear to see that she was miserable. As miserable as he was.

19

Nathan scrolled down the front page of a blog run by a researcher from the University of Cape Town. It contained mostly grainy cellphone pictures of Cape clawless otters spotted in and around Cape Town, some as far as Kommetjie and Pringle Bay. There were a lot of sightings in the Liesbeek River. Had Olivia come across any of these other hobbyists in her wanderings? Nathan looked for her name, but couldn't find any entries.

He studied a picture of an otter peeking out the water, its downturned mouth facing away from the camera. He could see why she liked them. They resembled puppies, with black glass-bead eyes.

It struck him that he was obsessing over otter blogs when he was trying to delete Olivia from his life. Instead of distancing himself from her, he kept finding ways to insert her back into his life, even with something as silly as looking at pictures of otters online. They reminded him of the old Olivia, the one who'd smiled whenever she saw him.

His phone vibrated on the desk in front of him. For one

hope-filled second he thought it was Mohendra, but it was only spam.

Putting his phone down, he continued staring at the pictures of the furry creatures on his screen. His finger hovered over the 'next' button, but he stopped himself from going any further.

What am I doing?

Nathan closed the browser window and switched off the screen. He was tormenting himself on purpose. His life was a mess. He'd lost Mohendra and Olivia, the only friends he had.

His bedroom was too constricting. Nathan stumbled across the floor to open his window and took a gulp of cold air. If only there was a way to pause his brain, to stop the world from spinning. He sideswiped his Aquaman figurine off the bedside table – the original Aquaman, not the Jason Momoa version. It didn't help.

He wished there was something he could do to expel the pain – cry, scream, smash something, but that would only be an outlet for his rage. The anguish would still be there to haunt him afterwards.

Nathan opened his laptop and watched a couple of episodes of the Japanese webseries that made its contestants do ridiculous things. In one episode, two contestants were tested on who could eat the most wasabi. It wasn't even funny, but just something to watch to pass the time. Mohendra had introduced him to the show. Thinking about his best friend instantly turned him off the series.

He checked his bookmarks for anything else to watch. It was annoying how one thing could so easily remind him of another, be it Mohendra or Olivia.

It was proving impossible to clear his head. The window

rattled against the wind, and he crawled across the bed to close it, noticing for the first time the turn of the weather. The window pane trembled under the force as he slammed it shut.

Once again his thoughts turned to Olivia, who was probably dancing under the neon lights in the community hall. Or was she? What if she was huddled outside, smoking a cigarette to please Virginie, or shivering from the cold beneath a tree while a bottle of something cheap and foul was passed around?

He clutched his head with his fingers, pressing hard against his temples. The worst part of it was knowing that he'd been fine without any friends. He didn't need people in his life. His entire school career had been based around that belief.

Only once had his shield slipped, allowing Olivia inside. Now he had no one and it was killing him. That wasn't supposed to happen.

His phone vibrated again, and he snatched it off the desk, ready to toss it across the room. But it wasn't spam this time. It was a WhatsApp message from Olivia.

Nathan lifted his hand slowly and brushed his fingers through his hair. He would delete the message without reading it, that's what he would do. His thumb hovered above the keypad, but he made no move to press it down. He couldn't. He had to know.

He swallowed and opened the message.

Help me. I'm too drunk. I don't know what's happening.

He stared at his phone for a total of four seconds before shoving it in his pocket. The community hall wasn't far away. He could reach it in under twenty minutes if he ran. He walked purposefully down the hall, passing the lounge, where his parents were watching television.

'Nathan, what's wrong?' asked his mother, sitting up.

'Olivia's in trouble and I'm going to fetch her.'

His father bounced to his feet and grabbed his car keys. 'I'll take you.'

Nathan met his father's gaze and felt the tidal wave of thoughts recede. He hoped his eyes conveyed his gratitude.

Dustbins and branches cartwheeled across the road, and plastic bags and leaves danced in clockwise circles. Any other night Nathan would have been transfixed by the storm's intensity, but his insides were frozen with panic.

'Left here,' he instructed his father.

'I know where it is, Nathan.'

Nathan sat on his hands to keep from fidgeting.

'Tell her we're coming,' said his dad. His voice was tight in his throat. In his own way, Nathan could tell that he was also really worried.

Nathan pulled out his phone. He hadn't thought to message her back. It was a stupid mistake. What if she was in more trouble because of it? He looked at his father helplessly, his tongue useless.

'Talk to me, kid. What's going on in there?'

'I'm scared,' he said. 'Worried.'

'We're almost there. Five minutes.'

The community hall was swarming with teenage bodies. The interior was lit up in bright purple and blue, giving the impression that the boring white building was breathing in and out.

Nathan's father pulled up into the parking lot.

'Wait here for me. The bouncers won't let you in – you're

too old,' said Nathan, jerking free of the seatbelt and throwing open his door.

The hall was packed tightly with teenagers. Nathan scanned their heads for Olivia. Shaun and a few other guys from school were standing against the wall and watching the girls dancing. He followed their gaze and immediately spotted Mandy and some of the other girls from the group. Olivia wasn't among them.

He ran back outside and began scanning the faces for hers. There were only two in the crowd he recognised – Virginie and Blaize. Virginie rested against the wire fencing, her arms wound protectively around herself. Her white-blonde hair shone like silver against her gold bomber jacket and made her stand out from all the other kids. There was a cigarette between her lips.

She looked up at him when he passed. There was no smirk this time, and not even a glimmer of recognition. She merely turned away like she didn't care whether he was there or not. Nathan wanted to rush up to her and pull that cigarette out of her mouth, throw it at her feet and demand that she tell him where Olivia was. But instead he veered left and ran along the side of the building towards the back, where the trees were denser and the light from the party didn't penetrate. He stumbled as he ran, his eyes adjusting to the darkness as he took in the couples littering the grass.

'Olivia!'

He searched the faces of those on the ground – they all had glassy eyes and slack-mouthed expressions from drinking too much. Each step made his heart pound in his chest. He had to find her. He had to.

He eyed a couple on the ground. She was lying on her back,

with her arms splayed – unconscious. The guy was kneeling over her, searching her pockets.

'Hey, leave her alone!'

The hooded figure took off, dropping Olivia's wallet to the ground. Nathan scooped it up and rushed to her side. She was passed out, but her clothes were all on and unruffled. He opened and closed his hands, unsure whether to touch her or not. But it was a momentary panic. He lifted her up by her arms and shifted her onto his shoulder. She weighed hardly anything.

No one tried to stop him as he carried her to the parking lot. When he arrived back at the car, his dad scrambled out to open the back door. A security guard watched them warily, but his dad said authoritatively, 'It's fine, it's fine, she's with us.' The security guard nodded and walked away.

Together, Nathan and his dad manoeuvred Olivia into the back of the car. One of her pumps had fallen off, and Nathan tucked in gently into her lap.

'She's not made of glass, son. She's just drunk.'

Nathan stared at his father. Music thumped softly in the background above the muffled laughter and the shouts of the partygoers. His father was nodding to himself, wrestling with a decision. His greying hair was being blown in every direction by the wind.

'What are we going to do?' asked Nathan.

His father stared at Olivia passed out in the car and sighed. 'Take her home, make her drink coffee. Do you know where she lives?'

Nathan shook his head. 'I can hack into the school server to find out.'

His father laughed. It sounded hysterical. 'God, Nathan. Come on. Let's just go.'

As his father eased Olivia's unconscious body onto the couch, Nathan ran to the kitchen to fetch a bucket, so that if she got sick, she wouldn't mess all over the carpets.

When he got back, his first instinct was to check her pulse, but he could see her chest rising and falling softly beneath her patterned shirt, her hair covering her shoulders. She could have been asleep, but her breathing was too raspy, like she was struggling to breathe.

Nathan's father put a hand on his shoulder, and he flinched in fright.

'Don't you have some hacking to do?' his father asked.

Nathan had momentarily forgotten all about that. He was afraid that if he took his eyes off Olivia even for the tiniest moment, something would happen. His heart was still beating too fast.

'I'm sure she'll be fine. I'll be here.' His dad looked at him kindly. Nathan gave his father a grateful glance, then ran down the passage to his room.

As soon as he was out of the way, his parents started arguing. He could hear them from his room. Nathan flinched every time his mother's voice rose, hoping it wouldn't wake up Olivia.

He worked fast. It only took a couple of seconds to locate the school's IP address. He pinged it, just to be safe. If the school server was managed by an external hosting company, there would be firewalls in place to stop his progress, but he was in luck. He pored over the code on his screen until he found what he was looking for. The program that stored student information was old and easy to manipulate.

In minutes he'd called up the code that contained Olivia's information. Olivia February. 17 St Georges Street, Mowbray. He was surprised at how close they lived to each other. He envisioned her house in his mind: a humble one-storey with a low vibracrete wall and clusters of blue and purple hydrangeas lining the driveway. He'd walked past it before.

He scribbled her address on the back of a scrap piece of paper and also noted down her mother's telephone number for his dad.

Nathan's parents stopped arguing abruptly when he re-entered the lounge. He couldn't quite read his mother's face. She was angry, yes, but there was something else there too: worry.

His father took the piece of paper, shaking his head as he read it. 'One day you need to show me how you do this. Where did you learn to hack into computers?'

Nathan shrugged. 'It's easy.' It was.

His father laughed and scratched the top of his own head. 'Well, I've made some coffee. Black. Let's get the patient on her feet.'

'Do we really need to wake her?'

'I'm afraid so.'

Nathan approached Olivia slowly and gave her shoulder a tentative shake. She didn't stir. His hand hovered above her. He hated the idea of disturbing her.

His father came up behind him and shoved his hands under her arms. 'There's no point dancing around her. We have to get some coffee in her.'

Once he'd lifted Olivia into a sitting position, he gave her a vigorous shake. Nathan resisted the urge to swat his father's hands away.

Olivia began to moan.

'Oh dear. I think we should get her to the bathroom,' his father suggested.

Carefully, they tried to hoist her up. Olivia opened her eyes blearily and Nathan's dad pushed him out the way just as she opened her mouth, unleashing a stream of vomit onto the couch.

'Quickly, grab the Handy Andy before it sinks into the fabric.'

Nathan hurried to the kitchen and searched the cupboards for the detergents and cloths. His mother was sitting at the counter, her hands curled around a cup of coffee. 'Might as well drink it, since we made it,' she said, her eyelids drooping and her mouth a tight line.

There wasn't time for Nathan to interpret his mother's strange expression. He grabbed the Handy Andy and a damp cloth, and left the kitchen.

Olivia was leaning on his father's shoulder, breathing heavily, while his father tried to coax her into drinking the coffee. So far, he'd only succeeded in getting her to hold the cup. Nathan dropped to his knees and began scrubbing the vomit off the couch. He had no idea what she'd been drinking, only that it was pink and smelled foul.

He heard his father's words above him. 'Come on, darling, drink this. You'll feel better.'

'Let me try. She doesn't know your voice,' said Nathan.

He dropped the smelly cloth into the bucket and took his father's place on the edge of the couch. Olivia's half-closed eyes tried to focus on him. The effort was making her sway back and forth.

'Here,' he said, pushing her hands holding the cup closer to her face. 'It's coffee.'

Something inside her pickled brain recognised his voice. She raised the cup to her lips and took a sip. His father gave him the thumbs-up sign.

Nathan exhaled in relief.

He reached for a tissue from the box on the coffee table next to him and wiped the vomit from her shirt. After she'd finished the coffee, she slumped against him.

'Olivia. Are you alright?'

She didn't answer. She'd just passed out again. Nathan looked at his father in panic. 'Should we take her to the hospital?'

'I don't think so. She's obviously just not used to alcohol, and luckily she's thrown up most of what was in her stomach. Hopefully we can get her to sober up and still get her home before the sun comes up.'

Nathan moved Olivia's sticky hair out of her face so that when she woke up, she didn't freak out about her appearance.

The house had never been so awake so late at night. While Nathan sat perfectly still so as not to rouse Olivia, his father stood over a boiling kettle making more coffee, and his mother loaded the washing machine with the vomit-stained throw that had been covering the couch. All the lights were on, so the house shone as bright as a lighthouse among its sleeping neighbours.

By two o' clock they'd managed to revive Olivia to lucidity. Nathan's mother, who'd been worrying all night, finally went to bed while Nathan and his father took Olivia home.

Nathan waited in the car while his father explained to Olivia's mother and grandmother how they'd found her. They were all red in the face, everyone shocked and embarrassed by the situation. He hoped he didn't get blamed by her mom for her getting drunk, like he had for Mohendra.

While the adults spoke, he noticed that the house was different to how he remembered it. The hydrangeas were nothing more than dead stumps and the grass was overgrown.

20

More than anything, Nathan wished he could speak to Mohendra. All he wanted was to hear his best friend's quick voice, always so forthcoming with advice. His thoughts would quieten as his ears strained to follow the dialogue. Mohendra was always so sure of everything, so certain that his view of the world was one hundred percent correct. He would end his monologues with a wink, or shoot an imaginary nine-millimetre gun. Nathan would relax, because if Mohendra wasn't worried, then he didn't need to be either.

Without anyone to talk to, he was more confused than ever. He didn't want to go to school. The thought of not knowing what was going to happen between him and Olivia was driving him insane.

Nathan attempted to divide the cut-up fruit on top of his Jungle Oats into different clusters based on colour so that his bowl resembled a puzzle. He should've finished breakfast already, but he found himself stuck to his chair, obsessing over the task.

His mother entered the kitchen and did a double take. 'What are you still doing here?' she asked.

He looked up. 'I don't want to go to school.'

'Are you sick?'

He shook his head.

She took a seat next to him. 'Things are never as bad as we make them out to be,' she said.

'There's no scientific evidence to back that up,' he replied stonily.

'Well, it always makes me feel better if someone tells me that. Do you want to stay home? I'm sure I can wrangle something.'

'No. I would just have to go in tomorrow anyway.'

She stood up to put on the kettle. 'There isn't enough coffee in the world for these types of mornings. I tell you what: if it gets too much today, text me and I'll come fetch you. We're all allowed to have bad days.'

'Thanks, Mom.'

He watched her clatter inside the dishwasher for cups. He'd delayed leaving long enough.

Nathan arrived at school wanting to get his first interaction with Olivia over and done with, so that he knew what to expect for the rest of the day. He needed to know if they were talking again, if they were still ignoring each other, if nothing had changed, or if everything had changed.

The idea of making the opening move terrified him. He sat in his first class, fidgeting in his seat, while he watched the door. But after almost fifteen minutes of waiting, only the elderly Mrs Booysen had arrived, closing the door behind her and calling for quiet.

Olivia was never late. Nathan continued to stare at the door while everyone else slowly unpacked textbooks and stationery boxes to start the lesson.

'Mr Langdon, is there anything I can help you with?' asked Mrs Booysen, her eyes narrowing behind her thick glasses.

Nathan shook his head and grudgingly bent down to get his own books out of his bag.

Olivia didn't come to that class. Or the next one. Her absence only made the new rumours circulating about her multiply. Nathan heard her name mentioned several times by girls refusing to keep their voices down, often accompanied by laughter.

That girl Olivia gets around, if you know what I mean.

One guy after the next.

Trash, that's what she is.

The blatant untruth of it made Nathan angrier than ever. More than once, he noticed Mandy or Jill's gaze swing towards him, and he wondered if his name was also being mentioned in the lies going around. It wouldn't surprise him.

The rumours about Olivia had started with those girls. He was certain of it. Someone in that circle was threatened by Olivia's presence and was doing a good job of trying to oust her from the group.

Nathan felt a stab of guilt. It was his fault for not trying to talk Olivia out of trying to fit in. It was his fault for not turning her down in the first place.

When the bell rang, he slowly walked past Mandy's desk. The girls were still chatting animatedly.

'Remember how she was carrying on about the Cape otter or whatever? Poor Ricardo was so bored! And she kept repeating herself. Ha! What a freak.'

Next to her, Jill was bent over with laughter. But it was Virginie who answered, her soft voice clear and mocking, 'They make their holts in the reeds. They're so easy to find if you know what you're looking for!'

The rest of the group laughed hysterically.

'What the hell is a holt anyway?'

'She's one crayon short of a box, that one.'

Virginie's voice sounded triumphant. 'No one will want to go out with her now. Hey, maybe we should try and set her up with someone else – see how far we can take this.'

Nathan felt his cheeks burn. He knew that teenagers relished talking badly about others, as long as it wasn't them. And Virginie's actions dictated those of the rest of the group – they wouldn't have mocked Olivia without Virginie doing so first. This was typical of group behaviour.

Olivia had gone from being counted among the strong to being perceived as weak, all in a matter of weeks. Nathan felt even more responsible than ever. He knew. He'd known all along. He could've stopped it from going this far.

Walking home, Nathan forced his feet to turn right at the park that served as the halfway point between his house and the school. There was an uneasiness in his chest. This always happened when he broke routine.

He pressed his earphones into his ears and let the music distract him. For the hundredth time, his inner voice told him to turn around and go home. But it wasn't just his inner voice. He also spoke the words aloud. 'Turn around, turn around, turn around.'

He walked on.

In the daylight, Olivia's house was a bright peach colour,

although a little rough around the edges where the paint was flaking off. He entered through the small gate that creaked when he opened it, and crossed the driveway. His temples had started to throb from the pressure of the constant should-I-stay-or-should-I-go happening in his head. He walked up and down the driveway several times before finally stepping up on to the stoep.

When he rapped on the front door, it didn't feel like his hand doing the knocking: it belonged to someone far braver than he was. The Nathan Langdon he knew didn't take risks, didn't go to parties or visit girls. But that was a different Nathan Langdon, a Nathan that hadn't got to know Olivia February.

He counted eight wooden block panels in the front door before it was opened by a woman with dark hair streaked with grey, tied into a tight bun. She stared at Nathan suspiciously.

He fought the urge to run. 'Is Olivia home?' he asked.

'Who's asking?'

He frowned in confusion. 'Me.'

Her expression darkened. 'I don't know you. And my Olivia doesn't keep the company of rude boys like you.'

She started waving her finger in his face, so closely that he had to take a step backwards. He had no idea what was happening.

'But you're the one being rude to me,' he said.

Her shoulders straightened in surprise. 'What did you say?'

He was baffled by the way their exchange had escalated so quickly, but subtlety was a talent he had yet to master. 'You're accusing me of being rude when all I did was ask a question. You're being aggressive for no reason.'

'You cheeky bliksem! Get off my property or I'm calling the police!'

He wondered if she was insane. She looked like she worried a lot. The lines in her face and dark rings under her eyes told him that. And, like Nathan, she looked like she sometimes forgot to brush her hair.

Olivia appeared behind her mother and tried to lead her away. 'It's okay, Ma. Nathan's a friend.' She rolled her eyes behind her mother's back. 'Just leave it, okay, Ma? Nathan is harmless.'

He wished he knew what she meant by that.

The door closed in his face and he could hear them arguing inside. He was just wondering how long he should stay, when the door opened again and Olivia appeared, blushing feverishly. She was wearing oversized baby-blue pyjama bottoms and a faded T-shirt.

'Hi, Nathan.'

'You weren't at school today,' he said.

'No, no, I wasn't.'

'Are you sick?'

She laughed in that infuriating way of hers that he couldn't decipher. 'Oh, Nathan. I've actually missed talking to you. No, I'm not sick. I just didn't feel up to going to school.'

He nodded. He guessed the reason she'd stayed home had something to do with what had happened over the weekend. 'Are you okay?'

She looked at the floor and he took the opportunity to study her face. She was smiling, but it was off. He didn't know what it meant. He wished he could see inside her brain.

'What happened?' he asked.

She looked up briefly, then down at the ground again, another sure sign that something was wrong. Then her smile disappeared completely. 'I don't really know what happened. Everything just fell apart.'

He knew from watching her that she'd been struggling to keep up the pretence of her act around the popular girls. But it was a lost cause, anyway. They didn't want her to succeed. He knew that, but did she? Did she even suspect?

'I'm ... I'm not sure what I did wrong,' she said tearfully.

'You didn't do anything wrong. Actually, no, you did. You changed because you thought that's what other people wanted. There was no way that could've made you happy.'

'But I wanted to be like them.'

'No, you don't. They're evil.'

She bit her lip, suddenly uncertain. 'Maybe it's my fault. I ruined everything.'

'No. I ruined everything. I told you what to do.'

They stood in miserable silence, both feeling equally sorry for themselves. He got the impression that they'd just had two different conversations.

'It's not your fault,' she said eventually.

The lace curtain flickered in the window. Olivia's mother was spying on them. He looked away. He hated the feeling of someone watching him.

'Do you want to go for a walk?' he asked.

Her eyes followed his to the window. 'Okay. Let me just go put some other clothes on.'

Nathan waited on the doorstep while she went inside to change. The sound of raised voices told him that her mother wasn't thrilled with the idea of her going out. He hated that he was overhearing such a private part of her life, so he pulled his phone from his pocket and pressed play on the Spotify app. He was on H now, which meant the first track that played was by How to Destroy Angels.

The soft instrumental music wasn't ideal for masking the sounds of the outside world. Grudgingly, he skipped till he found something louder. He hated skipping. It was just as bad as playing the music on random. The result was that he felt a little edgier, which always happened when he'd relinquished control over something. He was grateful to press stop when Olivia re-emerged wearing a pair of jeans and a lime-green jersey.

'My mom doesn't know who you are so she's being a pain,' she explained once they were heading down the road.

He shrugged. Olivia's mother was a pain, full stop. Nathan was finding it difficult to concentrate on having a conversation when he didn't know where they were going. They were walking in a random pattern, turning left and right with no apparent destination in mind. He was dangerously close to freaking out.

'What should I do, Nathan? Go back tomorrow and pretend everything's fine?'

He wanted to tell her about the rumours. He almost said something, but changed his mind at the last minute. 'I don't think that's a good idea.'

She spun around. 'But why? I can't just throw it all away and go back to being a nobody again!'

The words flew out his mouth. 'But they don't even like you.'

She blushed. 'Why do you always say the nastiest things to me?'

'What?'

She wiped her nose on her sleeve and looked away. 'Every time we hang out, you say something to hurt my feelings.'

He stopped walking. 'I'm so confused right now. I don't understand what you're saying.'

She rolled her eyes at the sky. 'And you don't even know you're doing it! You say things without thinking and you don't even notice when someone takes offence.'

'I'm sorry. I don't have filters like normal people do.'

'What does that even mean?'

'It means ... Nothing. Never mind. You won't understand.'

She glared at him and crossed her arms. 'You're doing it again!'

'What? Sorry. I didn't mean—'

'You've been ignoring me lately,' she said suddenly.

His mind jerked at the change of subject, and he opened and closed his mouth, floundering for something to say. 'I'm sorry. I was just trying to deal with ... with everything.' Why was he apologising to her?

Her expression softened. 'So are we friends again?'

The direction of the conversation momentarily stunned him. 'I have no idea. Are we?'

She laughed, and the panic that was helter-skeltering around his head receded. It couldn't be that bad if she was laughing. His shoulders relaxed. He had so much to tell her – about the rumours that were skyrocketing out of control and how Virginie was almost certainly the source of them – but he didn't know how. She always managed to turn him inside out when they were together.

Their feet took them to the same park he'd walked to before, with the Liesbeek Canal running through on its way to the river.

He wondered if his mind had subconsciously led him back there, because he knew she might like it.

They sat down under a tree, which provided shade from the afternoon sun. Nathan pulled a rectangular plastic pillbox out of his school bag that had a compartment for each day of the week. Olivia watched him curiously as he opened the first compartment and took out a bright red pill.

He offered her the box. 'Smartie?'

She looked down at the box, then back up at him. 'Did you really separate your Smarties according to colour?'

'Yes.'

She started to laugh, then stopped. Then she burst into tears.

He shoved the pillbox back into his bag. 'What just happened? Why are you crying?'

'I'm never going to be like them,' she wailed.

He reached for her hand, then thought better of it.

She dug up a small patch of turf with her shoe. 'What's wrong with me?'

'There's nothing wrong with you. How many times do I have to tell you that?'

'Then why don't they like me?'

He didn't know what to say. There were so many different reasons he could give her, but he was too scared to say any of them.

She wiped her nose. 'You do know,' she sniffed. 'You always know everything.'

'Have you ever considered that they might just be messing with you?'

She looked up and blinked back glistening tears. Her bottom lip wobbled.

His panic returned. 'Look, I'm not saying they are, this is only my opinion. I could be wrong. You changed the status quo. That could only ever go two ways – they could either accept or reject you. Virginie isn't the type of girl who accepts easily. That's not a reflection on you. It's in her nature. She has to be on top at all costs, and if you start rising up the ladder, she has to get you to fall.'

He babbled on, and Olivia started crying again. Nathan had no choice but to watch as her body shook and shuddered. He hated that there was nothing he could do for her. He didn't understand what was going on inside her head. He felt helpless.

When it became clear that nothing was going to cheer her up, he walked her home, hating himself for being so completely inept at being a human being. When she went inside, he waited for her to turn around and wave goodbye.

She didn't.

21

Dear Mohendra.

His fingers automatically deleted the words.

Hey.

No, that wasn't right either.

Hey, Mohendra. How's it going?

He shook his head and flicked his fringe out of his eyes. He'd never had so much difficulty sending a WhatsApp message before. All he wanted was to ask his best friend's advice about what to do. He was completely lost in unknown territory, the habitat of the emotional teenage girl. Only Mohendra would be able to help him. He was still a little angry, but his desperation outweighed his anger. If only he could force the words out of his fingers.

He decided to log on to Facebook to find out what Mohendra had been up to lately in the hope of discovering a conversation starter, but when he tried to search for Mohendra's name it didn't come up in his friends list. Mohendra had unfriended him.

Nathan stared at his screen as this information filtered through his brain. His best friend wanted nothing more to do with him. How was that possible?

He closed the application, and opened Discord. Mohendra had blocked him there too.

He leaned back in his chair. He hadn't realised that their fight had been that serious. He'd thought that after enough time had passed, things would work out. Clearly he'd underestimated Mohendra's anger. *Or maybe*, said the little voice in his head, *Mohendra wanted a normal friend.*

He spent the next few minutes checking other sites Mohendra frequented and noticed that he was still active on an online gaming forum. He closed the page. He didn't want to be online any more.

His phone buzzed in his pocket and he pulled it out to see a message from Olivia.

What's going to happen tomorrow?

Nathan wished he knew what to tell her. He was really starting to fear her reaction to him not telling her about the rumours going around, but he couldn't bring himself to. He typed out a reply. *Things aren't as bad as we make them out to be.*

Her one-word reply was simply, *Okay.*

He didn't know if she was going to be okay. He didn't know anything.

If Olivia hadn't slept at all the night before, then Nathan had hardly done any better. He was so flustered that by the time he started walking to school, he hadn't even tucked in his shirt or tied his left shoelace. He didn't know what to expect. Everything was up and down with them.

They were talking again. That was one fact he could hold on to. Everything else was a giant question mark that hung in the air.

He half walked, half jogged through the gate. Some of the grade 10 boys nodded in greeting as he passed. He waved back hurriedly before disappearing through the front entrance.

Boys don't wave, said the voice in his head.

Shut up. I don't care.

Olivia was standing outside the English class, nervously chewing on her hair. Her shoulders sagged when he approached.

'I don't want to go in there.'

'You have to. They'll mark you as absent if you don't.'

She twisted her plait between her fingers. Her eyes were big and moist. 'I should just change schools.'

Seeing Olivia in such a state made him feel like he was drowning. He felt worse than helpless. He wished he could hug her, but he couldn't. He felt useless.

Students passed them on their way to class. Some seemed to look at Olivia with interest. Nathan hoped that it was just his imagination. Surely the rumours hadn't spread across the whole school yet?

Olivia didn't seem to notice. She was staring into the classroom like it was a portal into her worst nightmare.

'Come on,' he said, walking in.

She followed slowly, but rushed to her desk as soon as she was through the door. Some of the girls laughed, which Nathan knew wasn't only his imagination. Olivia noticed too, because she started playing with her hair again. She sent him a panicked look, and he felt the floor fall away beneath his feet. What could he do?

An unknown woman with dark hair tied into a top knot entered the class and smiled broadly at the students. 'Hello, everyone. My name is Miss Tomlinson. I'll be filling in for Mrs Booysen today.'

'Is she dead?' asked someone at the back.

The teacher laughed. 'No, she's on leave. If you have a question, please put up your hand.'

She pulled a clipboard from the desk drawer and Nathan knew that she was about to do roll call, an exercise that always made him feel awkward. His worse fears were confirmed when she cleared her throat, lifted her head, and called out, 'Andile?'

A stocky kid at the back of the class barked out, 'Here.'

Nathan was glad he wasn't first. When she got to his name, he simply raised his hand. To his left, Shaun put on a gruff voice and shouted 'Langdon!' A few students laughed.

'That's enough of that!' said Miss Tomlinson tersely. She cleared her throat again. 'Olivia.'

Olivia put up her hand timidly, which made the girls sitting behind her burst out in bitchy laughter. Her cheeks burned bright red, and she sank lower in her seat.

Miss Tomlinson, who wasn't used to the various personalities in the class, smiled. 'Care to share the joke?'

This only made the girls laugh harder. Jill, who'd always been friendly to Olivia, winked at the others and turned to the teacher. 'It's nothing, Miss. It's just we usually call Olivia "Otter". It's her nickname.'

Miss Tomlinson laughed.

Olivia picked up her bag and bolted from the class.

Nathan instinctively shot up too. 'Why do you have to be so nasty all the time?' he shouted at the girls, before running out after Olivia. He spotted her at the end of the passage. 'Olivia!' he called, and hurried after her, but lost her when she slipped inside the girls' bathroom.

He skidded to a stop and put his hand against the wall to steady himself. He knew he was guaranteed a backlash for his outburst but he couldn't help it. The way he felt about Olivia was making him act crazily. There was no way he could explain it to anyone, mostly because he didn't understand it himself.

Waiting outside the bathroom, he counted the bricks in the wall. *Twenty. Thirty. Forty. Fifty.* He was worried, but also clueless. He'd never been in a situation like this before. *Seventy five. Eighty.*

Ten minutes later Olivia appeared, red-eyed and miserable, a tissue clutched in her hand. 'Everyone hates me,' she said.

'I don't hate you.'

'You don't count.'

She sniffed and Nathan offered her a fresh tissue from the pocket pack he kept in his bag.

'I think I want to go home.'

He nodded and extended his hand to take her bag. It didn't matter that he was going to get into huge trouble. He was helping Olivia, and that was all that counted.

They left out the back entrance, which took them home via a longer route. Olivia walked slowly, hunched over, her eyebrows knitted closely and her mouth a thin, downturned line.

Nathan walked beside her in silence, carrying both their bags. He couldn't think of anything to say that would make things right. Walking her home was all he could think to do. He hated seeing her so miserable.

They arrived at Olivia's house in just over ten minutes.

Nathan hung back in case her mother was lurking behind the lace curtains again.

'It's okay, she's working today.'

He nodded and came forward, remaining a respectful distance behind Olivia, who was fumbling with her house keys. He noticed that some keys on the keyring were broken and had been replaced with new ones, and that she hadn't thrown the old ones away. He noticed these little things, and it bothered him. It bothered him a lot. Throwing the broken keys away would have saved her precious minutes every day. He didn't understand why she kept them.

He was still fixating on the keys when Olivia cleared her throat to let him know that the door was open and he could follow her inside. It was hard to shift focus after being so absorbed. He had to remind himself that this wasn't about him. This was about Olivia.

He entered the house and swore under his breath. The place was a mess. There were piles of old newspapers, envelopes from opened mail, magazines piled on every surface, several small boxes shoved under a coffee table. It was his worst nightmare. It gave him goosebumps.

He didn't want to move, but Olivia was walking down the passage and he had no choice but to follow.

'My mother doesn't like throwing things away,' she explained without turning around.

He didn't reply out of fear of saying something that would be taken the wrong way.

They entered her bedroom, which was, mercifully, neater than the rest of the house. He moved to the window and ducked his head under a large dreamcatcher to take a seat on the ledge.

This positioned him on the opposite side of the room from Olivia, who was pulling off her socks and shoes, and kicking them under the bed. There were printed-out photographs everywhere, some in black and white, others in colour – on the walls, on her cupboard doors, on the big mirror over the dressing table. Most of them were of her new friends, especially Virginie and Mandy. The pictures had mostly been taken at parties and had a slight grimy edge to them, as if she'd downloaded them from Facebook and Instagram.

She caught him looking and crossed the room to the cupboards and began tearing them all down, one after another. The more she took down, the angrier she got, until she was tearing the pictures down by the fistful.

He turned away and his eyes fell on a notebook on her bedside table with the words 'Olivia's Otter Log' written on the cover in her neat handwriting. So she'd started keeping a logbook after all. He wanted to hide it so that she didn't throw it away too.

She looked up and he quickly shifted his gaze so that she couldn't see where he was looking.

'I hate my life,' she said bitterly. 'None of this was supposed to happen.'

'I know.'

Her face scrunched up, and she lifted her hand, still clutching a photograph, to wipe a tear away.

'It almost worked,' he added.

She dropped the photos into the bin, but most of them spilled out onto the floor. He bent down to collect them.

'Why do you like me?' she asked, suddenly.

He looked up to see that she was staring down at him, a strange expression on her face, half miserable, half curious.

'Because you speak to me like I'm a normal person.'

It was the truth, but he could see that she hadn't been expecting it.

Nathan got up slowly. He wanted to go sit back down by the window and wait for her stormy mood to pass, but she grabbed him by the arm, just above his elbow, forcing him to turn around. He froze as she brought her face closer to his. He wanted to push her away, but he could never do that.

Her eyes were closed. She was coming closer. His fist tightened around the pictures in his hand. It was all he had to hold on to.

His only experience of kissing was what he'd seen in movies and comic books. He knew what to do theoretically, but once his face was enveloped by a crying, emotional Olivia, he was totally unprepared for it. Her lips forced his open, and she pushed her tongue into his mouth. He didn't know what to do, so he let her do all the work, swirling her wet tongue around. For a wild second he wondered if he was going to choke. Not daring to breathe, he kept his eyes open.

It was a long time before she stopped kissing him.

When it was over, he retreated back to the window to catch his breath. They stared everywhere but at each other. His heart was beating very fast and he wanted to ask her a hundred questions about what had just happened, but then her gaze fell on her otter logbook and her mouth twisted into a sneer.

She made a move to grab it, but he got there first and pulled it out of her reach.

'Don't.'

'Give it to me!'

'No.'

She jumped up, but he lifted the book higher.

'Don't let them change who you are. Then they win.'

She took one more half-hearted swipe at the book before slumping onto her bed and flopping down, face first. 'I hate otters now. I could never look at that stupid logbook again. They've ruined it. No, I ruined it. I'm just an idiot.'

'No, you're not. What are you even talking about?'

As he put the book back down, he noticed a loose slip of paper inside. It was a photo of an otter peeking out of a patch of muddy grass. Olivia must have printed it off the internet too. He pushed it safely back inside.

She smiled, which turned him inside out again. 'I didn't think I'd like you in that way,' she said.

He sank back down on the window ledge and stared at her. 'I don't know what's going on right now,' he said. 'I think I should go home.'

He stood up to leave and Olivia rose to block his exit, pushing herself against him. This time he was expecting it, and was able to react before her tongue lodged itself in his throat. It was still a wet, uncomfortable exercise, but it wasn't too unpleasant the second time.

22

Nathan enjoyed making lists. It was a good way to compartmentalise life. The best part about lists was that it helped him focus on one thing, while the buzz of everything else was reduced to a distant echo.

He made a mental list about Cape clawless otters.

1. They lived in fresh water, but their feet weren't webbed like the clawed kind.
2. They were mostly active during the day, but not at the hottest times.
3. Their favourite foods were freshwater crabs, frogs and eggs.
4. Their bodies were brown, with lighter patches on the chest.
5. Olivia wanted one as a pet.

The door opened and his father came in. 'Hey, kiddo. Have a minute?'

'Sure.'

He wanted to tell his dad about what had happened with

Olivia, but the voice in his head was so busy debating whether or not to say something that he didn't.

'I got a call from a Miss Tomlinson at the office today. She said you stormed out of class after being rude to some of the girls.'

'I could have been ruder.'

His father sighed. 'What happened? I thought I'd talk to you about it first before telling your mother.'

'They were bullying Olivia. I ran out of class after she did, to make sure she was okay.'

'Ah, Olivia. I see a pattern emerging.'

Nathan looked up in surprise. Seeing patterns was his speciality. If his dad was noticing things that he didn't, then his brain must really be broken. 'Did Miss Tomlinson tell you I didn't come back to class?'

'She did.'

He nodded. 'I'm surprised she noticed. I had to walk Olivia home.'

'That was very gentlemanly of you, but bunking school wasn't. I know you have a soft spot for that girl and she's making you do all sorts of crazy things, but you have to try and stay in control.'

Nathan swallowed and nodded. His father had just read his mind.

'I understand. I was the same at your age. There was this one girl, Lauren. I was mad for her, but ... Maybe I shouldn't tell you about that. Look, is there going to be a repeat performance?'

'No. It's just ... being around Olivia makes me a bit crazy. My brain stops working.'

His father laughed. 'That's what I thought. I told Miss Tomlinson that you'd probably been provoked.'

'She's new.'

'Ah, well. She'll learn.' His father patted him on the leg. 'Try not to get too carried away with this Olivia girl. I know your intentions are good, but try to think before you act.'

His father was about to leave when the words fell from his lips. 'She kissed me.'

His father halted at the door, his face unreadable. 'And how was it?'

Nathan considered the question. 'Awkward.'

His father nodded. 'You know, that's exactly what I thought you'd say.'

Nathan sent Mohendra an email telling him to stop being stupid and to come over to finish their game. He thought that maybe if he didn't apologise and pretended that everything was okay, then Mohendra would too.

Nathan lay back and continued working on his list. Thinking about otters was calming. He suspected this was mostly due to the fact they reminded him of Olivia, and he definitely didn't want to think about Olivia directly. Not yet, anyway. But at the same time it was impossible to not think about Olivia. It was true what he'd said to his dad. His brain ceased to function around her.

Despite his best efforts, his thoughts returned to the afternoon in her room. It had been a new experience, being that close to someone. The kiss had happened far too quickly. In fact, it felt better afterwards, thinking about it and reliving it in his mind, where he could slow things down and focus on the best parts.

Is this what he wanted? It was the start, yes. But the start of what? Olivia was an unpredictable creature. She'd completely upended his life and he was wading through the debris, trying to piece everything back together.

He didn't want to think about what was going to happen next but that was also impossible. His brain was an independent machine that continued to whir and calculate without him. It was maddening. He wished there was a failsafe stop button that he could push when his thoughts started barrelling out of control. Life would be easier then.

He pictured them sitting together for lunch like they used to. He would enjoy her company and hear her laugh at the things he said that she found funny. He would start watching her in class again, every day discovering new aspects to her that he hadn't noticed before – a birthmark behind her ear, or the tap of a foot to a song she was playing in her head.

He smiled to himself. Maybe his friendship would be enough to quieten that raging need she had for acceptance.

He went to sleep still thinking about her, and woke up several times in the night because his mind wouldn't stop. After a while he couldn't tell the difference between his thoughts and his dreams. They merged into one.

Nathan knew his parents didn't really understand him. They tried very hard to, especially lately. He was growing up. He wasn't the same strange child who'd left them puzzled and questioning their parenting abilities. He was outgrowing their influence, which he guessed his father was starting to realise. His mother was also starting to act differently towards him.

Regardless of the phonecall from Miss Tomlinson, his mother greeted him in the morning by kissing him on the top of his head. She didn't scold him or even ask him about it. This was a first. Usually she would want to know every detail, and then she'd try and talk to him about it. Whatever his dad had said to her had worked.

He left for school feeling lighter than ever. He should've asked Olivia if he could walk her to school. It was too late to change direction. She always got to school before him anyway.

He walked a little faster, suddenly eager to get there quicker. It was a sunny day, with a crisp breeze that gently grazed his skin, a sign that spring was coming.

Olivia stood at the front gates, her head thrown back in laughter.

A grin formed on his lips.

She was talking to a cluster of grade 11 guys. One hand was on her hip, and she was swinging her foot back and forth.

He smiled as he walked towards her. She turned and saw him, but instead of returning his smile, she turned away hurriedly and continued chatting to the guys like she hadn't recognised him.

Nathan's pace slowed. There was something about the way she'd turned her whole body away from him, leaning forward so that she was almost touching the guy next to her, that made him realise that something was wrong.

It was enough to make him quickly change direction and walk straight through the gates. He'd ask her about it in class. Maybe she was just in a hectic conversation and didn't want to be disturbed. But why was she being so rude to him? A hundred different scenarios whizzed through his mind. He remembered Virginie's words about setting her up with someone else and wondered if that was the cause.

When Olivia entered the classroom, she walked straight to her desk without looking at him, her head held high. She looked different again. Her black hair was pulled into a high ponytail, and her white shirt hadn't been tucked in properly. She sat straight up in her seat and crossed her legs slowly. The girls who'd made fun of her the day before elbowed each other and whispered fiercely.

Olivia looked at them and smirked before turning her head slowly and staring at the front of the class.

Nathan furrowed his brow. Whatever he'd been expecting, it was definitely not this. The emotional Olivia he'd walked home the day before was gone. This wasn't even the Olivia he'd coached to be more like the other girls. This was someone entirely different, someone he didn't know.

Even the girls could see that she wasn't acting like herself. Jill leaned forward and poked her hard on the shoulder. Olivia leaned across and smiled obligingly. When Jill spoke, Olivia merely laughed and turned away again. The girls shrugged at each other.

Nathan didn't want to make any rash judgements. He could feel a crushing disappointment beginning to twist in the pit of his stomach, but he didn't want to believe anything bad of her. She'd kissed him – twice. No one had ever kissed him before. No other girl had even spoken to him before. If there'd been a sign from the universe to prove that she liked him, then he couldn't have asked for more. So what was going on?

He kept looking in her direction in case she turned around. He didn't hear a single word of the lesson.

After class, she kept her gaze determinedly on the task of packing her books away. Nathan hovered behind her, but when she was done packing she walked off without turning back.

He stared after her for a long time before finally moving. This time the disappointment rose up willingly, and taunted him in his own voice. *You should never have trusted her.*

He stalked off, his shoulders bent under the strain of his own unhappiness.

He returned to his old spot under the tree to watch Olivia spend lunch with the same grade 11 guys she'd been speaking to before school. Nathan wasn't the only one staring at her. The girls in the group were glaring daggers in her direction, and Virginie wore a sour expression. Not having power over Olivia any more clearly annoyed her.

Nathan couldn't understand what had happened between the previous day and now. He didn't think he'd done anything wrong. But the negative script in his head reminded him that he probably deserved it for ignoring her before, and she'd said he always upset her, which wasn't really his fault, and was something he couldn't change. But it had to be his fault. He needed it to be.

It started after break, when Nathan was at his weakest, and most confused after spending half an hour watching Olivia spending time with the grade 11 boys. He was still torturing himself over what he'd seen when Mandy tripped him on the way to his next class. He lurched forward, but managed to stop himself from falling to the ground.

Everyone around him started laughing, which was the obvious intention of the attack. Virginie and her group wanted to strip him of his invisibility, make him into something to laugh at, just like he'd been during the first days of high school. But he knew that what they really wanted to do was make him pay for calling them out in class.

He knew Mandy expected him to shuffle away in shame, his eyes trained to the floor, and his instincts screamed for him to do just that. But he didn't want to. Not after everything he'd been through. He merely shook his head and walked on.

'Don't shake your head at me, freak!' Mandy shouted after him, then quickly added, 'Hey, I'm talking to you!' when he didn't turn around.

Loud and violent, that's all bullies were. He didn't put it past Mandy to push him or hit him, knowing he was powerless to strike back because she was a girl, but the possibility didn't frighten him. It was all posturing, like birds stretching their wings and opening their beaks to screech when another animal threatened their nest. And he knew that it wasn't really the girls who made fun of him, pulling their faces into ugly expressions, or trying to scare him by mock-attacking him as he walked past, who were to blame. It was Virginie – the slightly built blonde operator of her own personal terror machine.

All through that day they tried to taunt him, but he was numb to it. The shield he'd built around himself was impenetrable. The only person who'd ever found a way past it was Olivia, and the crushing disappointment he felt was worse than anything he'd ever experienced in his life.

Of course, that wouldn't stop Virginie from trying.

Nathan stared out the window as girls he'd never paid the

slightest bit of attention to before attempted to verbally bully him from their desks behind his. It was nothing but background noise to the crackling thundercloud of his mind.

Hey, Nathan, what's it like being a freak?

Don't people like him have to be in special schools or something?

Girls were bastards. If Mohendra was talking to him, he would've messaged him to tell him that he'd been right all along. But that was just another level to his misery.

The previous day had been the most incredible day of his life. In just twenty-four hours it had plummeted into his worst.

He walked home with his heart broken for the second time. Olivia had ignored him the whole day. He didn't understand what had gone wrong between them. This was worse than the time he'd broken his arm, worse than the resounding silence from Mohendra. This was a pain deep inside him that he couldn't reach.

The sound of running feet made him turn around. Olivia was skipping up to him, a huge smile on her face.

'Hey, wait for me.'

He stopped, and the bitter disappointment in his gut stopped twisting for a moment, just long enough for anger to take its place.

'Do you want to come to my place?' she asked, between gasps as she recovered her breath.

He stared at her in disbelief. 'Why, so you can ignore me some more?'

Her smile faltered. 'What's your problem?'

He inhaled sharply. 'You were really rude to me today. You didn't say hello or come talk to me once!'

Olivia laughed. 'Oh, Nathan. You're being oversensitive. Let's just go to my place, please. I'll explain everything.'

She reached for his hand and swung it back and forth, like a kid.

He wanted to believe her. His thoughts raced, confusing him, making him want to shout. 'Okay,' he said, between gritted teeth.

She grinned. 'Yay.'

At her place, sitting on her bed together, he asked again, 'Why did you ignore me today?' hoping that this time she would actually answer him.

He caught the quick look of uncertainty on her face before it disappeared. She bit her lip in what he supposed was an attempt at flirtation. She was doing it to avoid answering his question.

'Stop it, Olivia.'

'Stop what?'

'Stop pretending that you can't hear me. Why can't you be more like you?'

'But this is me,' she said, still chewing on her bottom lip.

'It's not.'

She flashed him a cute, toothy smile and moved in to kiss him. He had no more bed to back away into.

'Stop running away,' she squealed, half laughing.

He began laughing too, because her joy was that contagious. It was like magic, the way his unhappiness just disappeared into thin air. That entire day, which had felt like the longest of his life, dissolved as well. All that existed was that moment with her, where they were both content and everything was perfect.

Olivia had changed again. She was her old self again: playful, sweet. She even suggested another excursion to look for otters.

She didn't mention her bizarre behaviour at school, even after she'd told him that she was going to explain.

Nathan returned to school the next day expecting everything to be fine again. But just when he thought the worst was behind him, Olivia went back to ignoring him.

It struck him that she wanted to keep their relationship a secret. She might even be ashamed of it, a thought too horrible to contemplate. Nathan wanted to talk to her about it, but he couldn't articulate his thoughts. Whenever she was around at school, he lost the ability to think and speak, and he followed her blindly, looking at her from across the room while silently his misery festered and grew. He couldn't concentrate in any of his classes. His mind raced. His fidgeting increased.

Even though they'd kissed for what felt like hours the previous day, it hadn't been what he wanted. When he'd first met her, before any of the other stuff had happened, she'd made him feel normal. Fooling around in secret made him feel more abnormal than ever. He was her dirty secret, something to be ashamed of.

23

Olivia wound the headphone cord around her finger over and over, first clockwise, then anticlockwise, until Nathan had to look away.

Many unspoken words passed between them.

They were lying on her bed, facing each other, with their legs dangling off the end.

Being in her proximity was addictive. He enjoyed staring at random bits of her: an elbow, a shoe half on, half off, the way pieces of her hair floated at the back of her neck like they'd been zinged with some electrical charge.

But her closeness, as soothing as it was, wasn't enough. She hadn't spoken to him at all that day at school, and once again he'd been forced to watch her talking animatedly to other guys while all the time wishing she was talking to him. As this thought skulked above him like a dark cloud, she leaned across the bed and surprised him with a kiss. His chin jerked up, in time to see her radiant smile, before her lips, still curled in a grin, fell on his. The cloud evaporated with the kiss.

He needed to latch on to these moments with her. Whenever they parted, their time together came to seem unreal, like it had never happened. His doubts polluted the few hours he had with her, but he wanted what they had to be perfect. It gnawed at him that it wasn't. But whose fault was that? At school she behaved like she didn't care about him, while outside of school she was his entirely. The two Olivias didn't add up to one individual.

'What are you thinking?' she asked, when she pulled away.

He looked down at the duvet, his eyes following the lines of the flower stems printed on the material. 'Nothing.'

She laughed. 'You can't be thinking about nothing. It's impossible.'

He wished it was.

She nudged him on the shoulder with her head. 'Tell me,' she said.

He shifted away from her. He wanted to tell her that he was sick of the way she was treating him, that he didn't want to meet her in secret any more. The words sailed around his head in circles. He wanted to tell her about Mohendra's continued silence, which deepened the hole inside him every day. But he couldn't. He couldn't show her that he needed her. Need was just another form of weakness.

'Fine, don't tell me,' she said, flopping down onto her elbows.

He stared at her helplessly. He'd always been uncomfortable with personal contact, but their newfound closeness made him feel bold. He reached out and touched her arm with the tips of his fingers, desperate to be near her. He hoped the action conveyed some of what he was thinking.

Her skin was soft and the downy hairs stood up when his fingers passed over them. He could've run his fingers over her forever, but was forced to stop when her nose ploughed into him, pushing his head up to kiss him again.

How could she want this when her actions at school said otherwise? He didn't understand. Why kiss him in secret? If she wasn't interested in him, she wouldn't want to kiss him at all. That was his understanding of how attraction worked, but their relationship was far from normal.

He stroked her hair, which was still orange in places despite her efforts to dye it back. He wanted to ask her why she'd dyed it in the first place, but her sudden transformations were on the list of topics they didn't talk about. She preferred kissing to talking, and if that's what she wanted, he didn't want to ruin it.

Before this, she hadn't changed that much during the years he'd known her at Conradie High. She'd never dyed her hair or deviated from the tight braid she'd worn. It was only recently that she'd felt the need to transform herself.

Her dyeing her hair wasn't part of the advice he'd given her. He preferred it the way it had been, but Olivia was determined to run away from her old self. Nathan hugged her, thinking that if he held on tightly, less of her would disappear.

'Do you ever wish you could be someone else?' she asked, looking up from his shoulder.

'When I was a kid I did, but I stopped doing that.'

'Why?'

He thought about it for a while. 'Because I think everyone is equally unhappy on the inside.'

'I've never thought about it like that. I like the idea of there being someone out there happier than me, with a life I could just slip into.'

'But if you still had your own mind, wouldn't your unhappiness just go with you into the new body?'

'It's just pretend, Nathan.'

'Oh, okay. Then I want to be a mutant. Or Thor. Thor would be good.'

She laughed. 'Maybe I would be Katy Perry, then. Katy Perry with pink hair.'

Olivia with pink hair. That would be weird.

Nathan wondered what had triggered her desire to be popular. Her father leaving? He leaned across and kissed her lightly on the forehead. The action gave him a bold thrill. 'Are you happy right now?' he asked her.

She looked up. Her eyes were hazelnut in the waning afternoon light. 'Yes. Are you?'

He nodded.

'I'm glad. Everyone deserves to be happy.'

Her smile vanished. He wished he could travel inside her mind and fix the wiring so that she never felt sad again. Too bad people weren't as easy to repair as robots.

He left her as soon as her mom got home. He needed to get home anyway. His mother didn't like him coming home late, so he tried his best to get back in time for dinner. It meant that he had to do his homework much later, but he preferred it that way. It left less time to question his and Olivia's relationship.

24

Nathan wished he could leave his mind at home. It would mean less effort trying to get through school without upsetting himself. He thought about the previous day's visit to Olivia's house, replaying the good moments: her smile, her laugh, her kisses. Those memories shielded him from the sight of her performing for the older guys and the constant taunting that followed him everywhere.

The girl he saw, in her short skirt and with her dyed hair, wasn't his Olivia. His Olivia belonged to him and him alone. She was in there somewhere, or maybe she only existed after school.

He was so preoccupied that he'd forgotten his lunch at home. He'd taken it out of his backpack that morning, to repack his books. He could see it on the bed where he'd left it. Luckily, going to the cafeteria spared him having to watch Olivia with those guys.

He joined the line behind Shaun, who was still being friendly to him.

'Howzit, Langdon,' said Shaun, play-punching him on the shoulder.

'Hey, Shaun.'

'Do you play fantasy football? I bet you play fantasy football.'

'No.'

'You should. Some of the guys have a league going. I bet you'd kill. It's all about using your brain.' He tapped his temple.

Nathan nodded. Their conversation was edging dangerously close to awkward territory. Nathan scrambled for something to say. He and Mohendra could speak about games for hours. Well, Mohendra could talk for hours. Nathan wasn't used to starting conversations.

Luckily, Shaun couldn't be silent for very long. 'I started playing the new FIFA, which is pretty fun. I'm really good at the soccer games. But that's only when I have the time to play. I prefer real soccer, if you know what I mean? Me and a couple of guys used to play league every week, but everyone forgets or doesn't show up to play. You know how it is.'

Nod.

'I should probably just join another league.'

Nod.

Nathan peeked at his wristwatch. When he looked up he spotted two identical blonde ponytails near the front. Mandy and Jill had ventured away from the group. He watched them cautiously. Mandy noticed him staring and made a slack-faced expression by crossing her eyes and letting her tongue hang out. Jill erupted into laughter next to her.

Nathan looked away quickly, the heat rising up his neck. He shifted uncomfortably and refocused his attention on Shaun, who was still talking about his glory days in the league.

'This one night we played these massive okes and still managed to beat them four-nil. It was epic.'

Nathan nodded absently. He could still hear Jill and Mandy's laughter and was trying really hard not to show that he was affected.

Shaun grunted loudly. 'Now I feel like playing FIFA,' he announced.

Nathan looked at his watch again. 'You can in ninety minutes.'

Shaun slapped him on the back. 'Good old Langdon. You're a legend.'

Out of the corner of his eye, Nathan noticed that Jill and Mandy had left to rejoin the ranks. He hoped they weren't getting bored of tormenting him. If their attention was focused on him, then Olivia was safe.

Nathan waited outside Olivia's house for her. It would've been so simple for them to walk home from school together, but she was even against that.

He stood awkwardly in the front garden, swinging his backpack back and forth, counting down the minutes in his head. She arrived seventeen minutes later, her face showing the telltale signs of misery – red eyes and an unhappy pout.

'What's wrong?' he asked.

'Virginie is spreading a rumour about me – about us.'

He frowned. 'What's she saying?'

'That we're secretly dating.'

She said it with such venom that he took a step back. 'So what?'

'So what? It's embarrassing. I hate her. I hate her. I hate her!'

He stared at her while she fumbled with her set of broken keys. His heart beat very past. 'What's the embarrassing part?'

She spun around and flicked hair out of her face. 'What?'

'What are you embarrassed about, the rumour or the part about dating me?'

She froze, the key halfway to the door. 'That's not what I meant.'

'Then explain what you meant.' His body shook from the conflicting emotions inside him. Anger, confusion, hurt.

She looked away, shaking her head, and attempted to open the door. When she failed to find the right key, she threw the bunch to the floor with a frustrated grunt. 'I've had a really bad day, okay? Can you come round tomorrow rather? I need to chill out.'

'Whatever.'

He walked away, not bothering to say goodbye. He was so angry with her. It seemed impossible for her to consider his feelings, but worse than that, she couldn't see that he really, really liked her. He couldn't imagine that she would treat him so cruelly if she knew that. He didn't understand why she was so upset over a stupid rumour. There had been plenty of rumours. What was so wrong with the idea of dating him?

He stalked home, replaying her words in his mind, feeling more like that-weird-kid than ever before. Because honestly, what other reason could there be for Olivia's embarrassment?

25

Nathan sat in the back living room, facing the double doors, and watched the rain run down the glass. It was a miserable Friday evening, with black clouds threatening the suburbs from their vantage point above Table Mountain.

He'd cancelled his and Olivia's trip to go otter-spotting that afternoon, for two reasons. One, because of the danger of slippery banks and an overflowing river. But, two, because it was one way in which he could rebel against their screwed-up relationship.

He doubted she would pick up on the hint, though. Olivia was on her own mission and was making up the rules as she went along. She'd lost her footing with the popular girls, but was leveraging her new reputation as a party girl to hang out with the older guys at school.

Now that he'd had some time to think about it, Nathan could see that it was a wild move, and also a desperate one. She wouldn't be able to sustain her new behaviour. As much as she thought she was being one of the guys, there would come a time when they would want to do something else during break time that didn't involve her, like play soccer, or someone would get the wrong idea and try and make a move on her.

And no one knew about their relationship. Nathan wasn't sure about it himself. It had started out as a tenuous friendship, and now it involved kissing. They weren't dating – that had become glaringly obvious. No, the rumour was an unlucky coincidence that seemed to have sunk into Olivia like an arrow.

If Olivia wanted to date him, she would've said something. She was the type of girl who went for the things she wanted. She didn't wait around to consider the options like he did.

His laptop was open next to him on the couch, but he didn't go online. He couldn't do anything. He'd even thrown away his robot. He just wanted to stare at the wet world outside and let his mind wander.

His mother walked into the room and stopped short. 'Nathan, why are you sitting in the dark again?'

He hated that his mother had this magical ability to find him when he didn't want to be found. 'I'm watching the rain.'

'In the dark?'

'It looks better when it's dark.'

She dropped onto the couch beside him. 'This is about Olivia, I assume. Want to talk about it?'

He shook his head and pulled up his legs and tucked them underneath himself. He wished Mohendra was around to take his mind off his troubles, but his ex-best friend still hadn't replied to his email.

'You must be missing Mohendra, huh?' his mom asked, reading his mind with the same super-power his dad possessed.

'He doesn't want to be my friend any more.'

'Why not?'

'I don't know.' Saying it out loud made him feel worse.

'Have you messaged him lately?'

'Yes. Sending another would just look like I'm grovelling.'

'Do you want me to call his mother?'

'No. That's a terrible idea. But it would be nice if you told me what you said before about things not being as bad as we make them out to be.'

'Oh, sweetheart. I'm sure it'll work out. Friends fight all the time.'

Yes, he thought, but Mohendra was his only friend. He could never find another Mohendra, just like he could never find another Olivia.

His mother put her arm around him.

He stiffened. 'I'd like to be alone, if that's okay.'

'Of course.'

His stomach growled for food. He'd skipped dinner. He had the same inexplicable disinterest in food that had stopped him from putting on the light. He just wanted to sit there, lost in the world of his mind, until his life started making sense again.

Olivia hadn't responded to his text cancelling their non-date, which was another indication that she didn't give a damn about him.

He didn't understand what he was feeling. The way she was treating him should've made him like her less, but that stupid hope that they would find their way together still remained. There was nothing in her behaviour that fed that hope. It was all his own desire.

He had to say something to her, even if it meant losing her. If he didn't, then nothing would ever change between them.

Mind made up, Nathan grabbed a jacket from his room and left the house. A soft rain was falling, and it didn't take long for his hair to stick to his neck. Despite getting drenched, he didn't quicken his steps. He wanted to drag out the walk for as long as possible.

No one else was out in the soggy streets; it was just him and the scents of other people's gardens washed into the air by the rain. If he and Olivia had been dating, he would've picked some flowers along the way, some roses, a bunch of jasmine hacked from an overgrown bush, and whatever else was growing over fences and garden gates. But they weren't dating, so he didn't.

He stopped outside her house and changed his mind about six times before actually unlatching the gate. At his knock, her mother opened the door and narrowed her eyes when she saw who it was.

'Olivia's not here,' she said, with a flick of her head.

'Did she go otter-spotting by herself?'

He felt a stab of guilt for cancelling. It was raining. The banks were probably slippery. He hoped she was okay. He should go look for her.

'No, she hasn't been home yet. Her friend Ricardo picked her up last night for a party and she said she was going to stay over at her friend Mandy's house.'

Ricardo was one of the grade 11 guys Olivia had started hanging out with at break. So clearly his prediction that someone was going to make a move had turned out to be true.

Nathan stared at the buttons on Olivia's mother's dress. There were six in total. They were red and dull. They took up the whole world. He didn't want to look away.

She clicked her fingers in front of his face to get his attention and he jerked awake.

'Thank you,' he mumbled.

That cold feeling was back, but this time it seeped into his bones. Olivia and Mandy were no longer friends. He was one hundred percent sure of that. There was no way that could've changed overnight. So she was with Ricardo, and wasn't planning on coming home, which is why she'd lied to her mother.

He remembered overhearing what Mandy had said about Olivia flirting with Ricardo at a party. So she hadn't bored him with her otter talk, after all.

Nathan trudged home, because he had nowhere else to go. He couldn't exactly show up unannounced on Mohendra's doorstep, especially after Mohendra had gone to such lengths to cut him out of his life. He had only himself for company. At least there was one advantage to that: he couldn't betray himself.

He was sodden by the time he unlocked the front door. He went straight to the bathroom to run a bath, which he hoped would get rid of the coldness inside him. A brief thought flitted into his mind, that maybe he should give Olivia the benefit of the doubt, but he disregarded it immediately. He'd gone to her house to demand a reason for why she was doing this to him, and now he had even more proof of her cruelty.

His fingers trembled as he untied his shoelaces. Why would she go out with Ricardo and not with him? Ricardo didn't seem the type of guy who made friends with girls. He had a group of guys he hung around with, and he only ever spoke to girls so that he could flirt with them. Maybe Shaun was right that

Olivia had a reputation. Maybe she wanted people to think that so she could be popular with the older guys.

He stepped into the hot water and sat down. He was shivering badly. If only getting this pain out of his system was a simple matter of tearing some photos down off the wall.

He remembered the anguish on her face. He wanted to take it away so that she could be happy again. He realised with a pang that he wasn't enough to make Olivia happy. He would never be.

He let himself sink down into the water. He never used to have a problem with his feelings before. Now he had too many and he didn't like it. He hated that his state of mind was influenced by another person, that his happiness and sadness were reliant on her actions. If this was what being in love was like, then he didn't want to feel it ever again.

He would build another shield, a thicker one, that's what he would do.

Forty minutes later Nathan's skin was as wrinkled as an old man's. Still brooding, he returned to his room.

As he lay in bed, the familiar cold pain of disappointment settled on him, gluing him to the spot. He couldn't move and it became an effort to breathe. It felt like there was a heavy weight on his back, crushing him. Liking someone wasn't supposed to be like this. It wasn't supposed to hurt this much.

What had he thought was going to happen? That Olivia would give up everything she wanted to be with him? The idea felt so stupid now.

Nathan spent the rest of the weekend in his room, listening to music, playing games on his laptop, watching television series, working out – anything he could do to keep his mind occupied.

He didn't hear from Olivia. He wanted to send her a message more than anything in the world, but he couldn't bring himself to do it. If she wanted to get in touch, she would. It was obvious that he was the last thing on her mind. Messaging her would just make him look desperate and needy.

He was dreading school on Monday, and despite his wish for a supernova to wipe out the world, the new week was coming at him full force. The thought of seeing Olivia, dressed all wrong, was too much. He would give anything in the world to get the old Olivia back, but even that version of her felt wrong.

He wondered if he hadn't just built her up to be this perfect girl in his mind because he'd wanted to believe that people weren't as bad as he thought, that some could really be trusted.

G_Nat. You alive?

The Discord message from the player Pants_On_Head flickered on his screen. Nathan had logged on to DOTA to try and get his mind off everything, not talk to people.

Earth to G_Nat?

He killed the screen. He couldn't do it.

When his father came to check on him, he couldn't find the words to explain what he was feeling. He didn't even know what to say. It was too much to speak.

26

It churned up his insides to see that Olivia was happy again and smiling all the time. Nothing anyone said could touch her. She was above it all, exactly where she felt she should be. And that was the problem. It was the result they'd both wanted, but it wasn't the right one. It was wrong. Wrong, wrong, wrong.

Nathan watched her like a naturalist studying a wild animal that kept biting. She was proud and beautiful and untouchable. She wasn't the same person any more.

She laughed at something someone said and turned around. Their eyes met for a second. There was no guilt there, no remorse, no sadness. There was nothing there.

At least the coven of witches were leaving him alone, but it was a small consolation. He was broken.

At break Nathan forced himself to walk to the field to see for himself and to get some sort of closure. Olivia and Ricardo sat next to each other on the grass, grinning and smiling like old friends. The sight left him empty. That's where he was supposed to be. Not Ricardo. Did she know he was watching? Did she care?

He knew exactly why she was flaunting her relationship with Ricardo in front of everyone: she wanted to put an end to the rumour that there was anything between him and her. He glared in her direction. She didn't seem to mind that he was the one who would get hurt the most as a result of her display. They looked happy, but deep down he knew it was a chess move.

He wished he hadn't left his phone at home. Music would prevent the self-destructive thoughts from taunting him. He was forgetting more and more recently – another symptom of the disease called Olivia.

At home, after school, Nathan sat alone in his room, trying and failing to distract himself. His homework lay strewn across his bed in various states of completion. Every time he tried to concentrate on one task, his mind travelled back to break time, to Olivia and Ricardo sitting together on the soccer field. For the thousandth time he gripped his head with his fingers and pushed hard, trying to force the thoughts out. No matter how many times he did it, it didn't work.

When the screen of his phone lit up, he grabbed it.

Nate, can you come over? I need to talk.

Nate? No-one called him that, and Olivia had never called him that before. What did it mean? He considered the options, but was frustrated to find that he just didn't know.

He left his homework as it was and changed into a pair of jeans. He didn't care if he got in trouble for not doing his homework. That particular worry was tiny when compared to the building-sized one that currently plagued him.

Olivia was still wearing her school uniform, her shirt pulled out over the skirt.

He sat on the edge of her bed, listening while she talked on and on about Virginie's latest vendetta. His heart continued to break in his chest for every second that passed of her not talking about the real issue – them.

'She called me a bad word. Right in front of everyone. But does anyone care? No, of course not, because Virginie is so perfect and lovely.' She wiped away tears from her eyes, which were red and puffy from crying.

'That wasn't very nice of her,' Nathan agreed, coldly.

'No,' she sniffed. 'And I've never said anything bad about her.'

That wasn't strictly true, but it wasn't for him to tell her, not when she was as worked up as she was.

'She's just a racist bitch. D'you think that's why she didn't want to be friends with me, because of my skin colour?'

Nathan shrugged. 'Possibly. I don't have enough information to go on.'

He'd walked in the rain to get here. His hair was plastered to his skin and dripping into the neck of his shirt, making him shiver. She hadn't offered him a towel.

When she beckoned for him to join her on the bed, he did so without question, even though he didn't want to kiss her after he imagined she'd been kissing Ricardo. It was nice to just hold her, even though his wet clothes were going to leave damp spots on the bedding. Her skin was warm against his.

He closed his eyes and enjoyed the feeling of her warmth and her familiar vanilla-shampoo smell. It forced all other thoughts from his mind. He could lie like this for hours.

She sighed heavily in his arms. 'D'you think she's jealous of me for all the attention I'm getting?'

Her words sent a twinge of pain through him. 'Maybe. I don't know.'

She turned on her side and laughed. 'Ricardo says those otters I saw at Kirstenbosch weren't otters at all, but mongooses. D'you think it's true? I looked them up online and the bodies look the same. It's only the faces that are different. What do you think?'

He tensed up. Was she testing him by bringing up Ricardo? Or maybe she wanted to see what his reaction would be.

His grip on her slackened and he straightened up. 'I don't know, Olivia. I'm not an otter expert,' he said, adding, 'And please don't talk to me about Ricardo. I don't want to know.'

She pouted in disappointment. 'Are you still upset with me?'

It felt like a joke, really, the fact that she could actually ask him that after everything she'd done. He manoeuvred himself to the end of the bed. 'I need to go.'

She frowned and narrowed her eyes. 'But it's raining.'

'It was raining when I came over.'

He saw a flash of anger in her eyes, which confused him. He hadn't done anything to upset her. The opposite was true.

His facial muscles twitched as he struggled to keep in everything he wanted to say to her. 'I don't think the problem is me, even though you say I always make you feel bad or that the idea of being with me embarrasses you. You're the one being cruel.'

She opened her mouth in surprise, but he didn't stay to hear her response. He had finally said some of what he wanted to say. It was a relief to hear the words outside of his own head.

He left with a sense of pride, even if the rest of him was numb.

He found a surprise waiting for him when he got home: a shoebox on his desk, filled with his half-finished robot. He rifled through the contents and found all the components accounted for. He'd have to re-sort everything into the correct piles, so he could continue working on it, but that didn't matter. It was something to focus on, to make the hours disappear.

His dad came in, his glasses on the tip of his nose. 'It was in the linen cupboard.'

'I thought I threw it away.'

His father smiled. 'Nah. Your mother saved it from the bin. She figured you might want it back.'

A drop of water dripped from Nathan's fringe and splashed on the desk. 'I should change,' he said, more to himself than to his father.

'I should say so. Your lips are blue. Where've you been?'

'I went to visit Olivia.'

His dad checked the passage then lowered his voice. 'How are things going with her? Did you play hard to get, like I suggested?'

'I don't think she noticed. I must be doing something wrong.'

His dad's lips formed a tight smile. 'Leave her alone for a little while. She'll come to you if she misses you.'

'That's the problem, Dad. I don't think she will.'

'Then maybe it's time to cut your losses.'

'I don't think I have any other choice.'

27

Mr Nicholson was just starting to explain the principles behind analytic geometry when Craig entered, apologising profusely. The teacher adjusted his glasses irritably, and motioned for him to hurry up.

Craig was still apologising when he passed Nathan's desk and carefully dropped a note from inside his blazer sleeve.

Nathan stared at the piece of paper in front of him. Guys didn't normally write notes to each other and he hadn't spoken to Craig since Virginie's party. He placed the note inside his textbook and carefully opened it. He recognised the handwriting immediately as Olivia's.

We can't see each other any more.

He closed the textbook on the note and turned around to see if Craig was watching him. He wasn't. He was busy chewing on a bit of loose skin on his thumb.

Nathan guessed he'd rushed to class and hadn't had time to read the note when it was given to him. Still, it had been a risky move on Olivia's part, especially since she wanted nothing more than to keep their relationship a secret. But then, notes were anonymous. WhatsApp messages were not.

For Olivia, apparently the thought of engaging him in conversation was worse than their secret relationship being discovered.

If she'd felt guilty, she would've offered some kind of explanation. It was maddening. But that was Olivia. Nothing she did made sense.

His hands formed fists under the table. She hadn't said sorry, either. She'd just put an end to his misery without apologising for making him miserable in the first place.

'Nathan, is everything alright?'

His whole body was shaking. He couldn't speak. All he could manage was to shake his head.

Mr Nicholson was at his desk immediately, helping him to his feet. He grabbed Nathan's books and shoved them into his bag. 'I'll walk with you to the nurse's office.'

Nathan nodded. He didn't feel sick. He wasn't sure what he was feeling. Something was broken inside him and his brain had gone hazy, like he was walking inside a fogged-up dome.

In the sick bay, Mr Nicholson remained in the room while the nurse made Nathan lie down on what he assumed was a germ-ridden bed and took his temperature. 'His heart rate is a bit high.'

Mr Nicholson nodded, his hand over his mouth. 'Could it be a panic attack?'

The nurse didn't answer, but lifted Nathan's shirt and pressed the stethoscope to his chest. 'Does it hurt anywhere?' she asked him.

He shook his head.

She nodded and removed the stethoscope from around her neck. 'Leave him with me. If he doesn't improve in the next twenty minutes, I'll send him home.'

Mr Nicholson relaxed. 'Thank you.' He turned to Nathan. 'Hang in there, Nathan. I'll tell the other teachers that you're not feeling well.'

'Okay.'

It was the first time he'd spoken since reading the note. The words sounded gravelly in his mouth.

He lay on his back for half an hour, ignoring the nurse's occasional prodding. In the end she scribbled a note for him to say he could go home. She smiled expectantly, like he was supposed to be grateful or something, but he just took the note and left, hurrying through the hallways, hoping he wouldn't run into anyone.

This is how super-villains were born. Nathan realised that he'd never been so simultaneously sad and angry in his life. If there'd been a Doomsday button in front of him, he would've gladly pressed it and destroyed the world and everything in it. It was a good day for the world to end. He couldn't bear to endure another one.

28

Nathan concentrated on writing a walking algorithm for his robot. It was exquisitely complicated, and varied according to speed, direction and terrain. At the core of his algorithm was the centre of gravity, which had to remain constant. If his formula was correct, his quadruped robot would achieve omnidirectional movement. The tricky part was in the rotation, but it wasn't really a challenge if he applied his mind to it. It was all patterns and numbers and trajectories.

He hadn't left his bedroom the entire day, except to eat and use the bathroom. His hair felt a little greasy when he ran his fingers through it, but he couldn't stop. He was riding a manic wave, taking full advantage of the momentum. And he had a brand-new Raspberry Pi to tinker with.

His father popped into the room occasionally to admire his work, and once to suggest a trip to Canal Walk for a meal or a movie. Nathan promised his dad that they could go as soon as he was done. The task required intense concentration that couldn't be broken. His efforts earned him the title of 'my little scientist'. He liked the idea of his dad being proud of him.

It had been a week since Olivia had ended things between them. He'd forced himself to stop looking for her at school, to pretend that she wasn't in any of his classes. It was easy for her. It had always been easy to ignore him.

The anger hadn't abated. It was still there, growling under his skin like a trapped animal. But he was managing. He didn't know any other way to describe it. He could only continue living his life one second at a time and hoping that the pain would eventually go away.

He wasn't expecting to receive a WhatsApp message from her.

Party in Rondebosch. Can you come? I'm really sorry about everything and I need to see you.

Nathan frowned at the screen. What could it mean? Nothing this girl did made sense.

He hesitated before replying. There was a heaviness in his gut that he couldn't explain, and he was still jittery from spending so much time working on his robot. He was edging towards panic, which was definitely not a state of mind he wanted to be in around people. But this wasn't just any person. This was Olivia.

He sat on his bed, thinking about what to do. He was still fighting with his inner voice when he showered and changed, and was no closer to a solution when he stood in front of his mirror checking his appearance. It was getting dark outside, and he could hear his mother shutting windows and closing curtains. He was out of time.

What's the address?

21 Jones Street. Near the Spar.

He knew exactly where that was. 'I'm going out,' he said, from the front door.

His mother popped her head out the arched doorway leading to the lounge. 'Where are you going?'

'Out.'

He couldn't explain. How would they understand what he was doing when he didn't even know himself?

He walked in the direction of the main road, which was the quickest and most well-lit way to Rondebosch. It was chilly, and he dug his hands into his jacket pockets and bowed his head to protect his face from the wind.

Main Road was quiet and empty. The Anglican Cathedral and graveyard loomed ominously in the darkness, and Nathan hurried past them. It was an irrational, childish fear, and when he reached the traffic lights, he started laughing, grateful that there was no one around to see him.

He was still debating the WhatsApp message. Did it mean Olivia was ready to take their relationship public? Was the old Olivia he knew back? Did she miss him? The thought struck a match inside him, reigniting his hopes.

Jones Street was dark. Some of the streetlights weren't working, so the only light came from the windows and the floodlights outside a block of flats. Nathan hurried down the road towards the unmistakable sounds of a party happening at the end of the street. He kept to the pavement, his eyes on the ground to watch out for loose brickwork. The loud music led him straight to number twenty-one.

What was he going to say to her?

He slowed his steps and stood in front of the house. There

were several cars out front. The windows were dark, but music and laughter were coming from the back garden.

Something inside him told him that this wasn't a good idea. It was an unfamiliar twist in his stomach, but he knew what it meant. He shouldn't have come. This was a mistake.

He bit his lip, considering his options, and began to walk in small circles. He could go in and find her. He could message her to meet him outside. Or he could go home.

The sound of broken glass and raised voices rooted him to the spot. Whoever lived there clearly didn't mind people acting crazily on the property. It made him want even less to go inside. But Olivia was inside. What if she needed help? Maybe that's why she'd messaged him. He had to know.

Moving slowly, Nathan let himself in through the gate. There was a gap between the house and the wall leading to the back. He made towards it and almost collided with Olivia. Her face glittered from all the make-up she'd applied.

'Nathan, oh my God. You have to get out of here.'

Seeing her panic made him start to panic. 'Why? What's wrong? Whose house is this?'

She looked quickly over her shoulder, her ponytail swishing. 'It's Ricardo's. He and his friends sent you that message from my phone. Please. You have to leave before they see you.'

'I don't understand.'

'What don't you understand? They're drunk and they want to mess with you. You have to go. Now.'

When he stayed where he was, she stepped forward and pushed him. She smelled like wine. 'Nathan. Go home. It's not safe for you here. These guys are not your friends.'

He didn't like the look on her face. Her eyes were wide with fear.

'I came because you told me to.'

'Urgh. Nathan,' she hissed. 'Leave. Before someone sees you. You don't want to mess with these guys when they've been drinking. Can't you see I'm trying to protect you?'

He sighed. This was just another part of the rollercoaster ride of their weird relationship.

'I don't want to leave you here.'

'Nathan. Go.'

He looked at her for a long time. She was scared. He was sure of it. 'Is it safe here? Are there any adults home? Maybe I should hang around.'

Her eyes flashed dangerously. 'Nathan, I swear to God, if you don't leave right now, I'm going to scream.'

He took a step back. 'Okay, okay. I'll go. Just promise me that you'll look after yourself.'

She didn't answer. Her lips were pressed together tightly, like she was trying to hold in her tears. She jumped and spun around at the clink of a bottle rolling on the ground. 'Quickly,' she said, waving her hand at him.

With a shake of his head, he turned around. She didn't run after him, but he wasn't expecting her to.

Walking home, he was surprised at how unaffected he felt by the trap he'd almost walked into. He'd long ago cushioned himself against ridicule, but he should have seen this coming. Olivia had joined a group that wanted to torment him. It was inevitable. After all, to be accepted into a group, you have to be like them.

His mother's eyebrows rose when he re-entered the house,

but he hurried past her so he didn't have to explain his sudden reappearance. He just wanted to go to bed and close his eyes. He was tired from the walk, and hoped that as soon as he lay down, sleep would save him from the voice inside his head.

And, despite everything, he hoped that Olivia would be alright.

29

Nathan woke to find Olivia sitting on the edge of his bed and staring out the window. At first, he thought he was dreaming, but after he'd blinked away the last dregs of sleep, she was still there.

'Olivia?'

She turned toward him slowly. She was wearing the same clothes from the night before and her make-up was smudged around her eyes. All the glitter was gone. Her face was all wrong. She wore a hard expression he didn't recognise. It was something more than sadness. Defeat.

Using his hands, he propped himself upright and reached for his phone to check the time. It was just past seven in the morning. 'What's the matter? Why are you here?'

She didn't answer, but turned back towards the window. There were red marks on her neck.

'Olivia? Is everything okay?'

She was sitting too still. Slowly, he pulled off his duvet cover and crawled across the bed to where she was. She didn't flinch, didn't laugh at his racing-car pyjama bottoms that he should've thrown out years ago. She just sat as still as stone.

His heart sped up. 'You're making me worried.'

Her throat bobbed up and down as she swallowed. 'I don't feel anything,' she said.

Somehow, her speaking was worse than her silence. Her voice was broken and raw. The sound made the hairs stand up on his arms.

'What do you mean?'

'I should feel something. But I don't. I ... I just don't care. Almost like I deserve everything that happens to me because I don't matter. Nobody wants me. Nobody cares. So it's fine if bad things happen to me. You can't even call them bad things. It doesn't count if they happen to me because I don't count.' She looked at him with wild, red eyes. 'It doesn't matter.'

'What doesn't matter? You're not making any sense.'

She shook her head. 'Me. I don't matter. I'm nothing.'

'Don't say that!' He reached across and pried her hands from between her knees. She didn't resist. He held them tight. 'What happened? Why are you talking like this?'

She turned her gaze back to the grey sky outside and didn't answer.

There were more red marks on her shoulder. He leaned back to look at the other side. The sleeve of her vest was stretched and warped, like it had been pulled with force.

'Did someone hurt you? Was it Ricardo?' he whispered.

'It doesn't matter, Nathan.'

'It does matter. Tell me. Please.'

He studied her nails for signs of a struggle, like the detectives did on crime shows, but he didn't know what to look for.

The dirt under her nails could've been anything. He didn't see any blood.

'I guess I understand why you like to sit by yourself at school. People aren't very nice, are they?'

'What are you trying to tell me? Please, I don't understand. Did someone hurt you?'

'It doesn't matter. I'm used to people hurting me.'

Her words exploded inside him. 'No-one should be allowed to hurt you,' he said between clenched teeth.

'Bad things happen to people every day, Nathan. What makes me so special?'

He gripped her hands tighter, his heart racing. 'You are special.'

She closed her eyes. 'No, I'm not. I shouldn't even be here after how I treated you.'

'Olivia ...'

'I should sleep. Can I stay here for a while? I don't want to go home.'

He nodded and grudgingly let her hands go so that she could get into the bed. She didn't close her eyes immediately, but stared at the wall with the same unreadable expression.

Rage surged inside him. Even after everything she'd done to him, he didn't hate her. The thought of anything bad happening to her made him reel. But her words were confusing. She wasn't talking sense. He needed to know what had happened to her.

He collected his clothes and shoes from the cupboard, but waited for her to close her eyes before going to the bathroom to change. He wasn't sure what he was going to do. All he knew was that he needed to go back to Ricardo's house to see if he could work out what had happened.

Before he left the house, he scribbled a note that he stuck to his bedroom door with Prestik. *Do not disturb. Olivia sleeping. She doesn't want tea.*

As he walked, Nathan purposely kept his mind busy so that he didn't have to think about where he was going. He passed seven white cars, one red car, three black cars and one yellow bus, which started him counting diesel engines only, of which there were four. Next he started counting his own steps. When he reached the sign for Jones Street, he was on five-hundred and eight. Bizarrely, it took twenty-one steps to get to number twenty-one.

All the cars were gone. The only sign of the previous night's party was a half-empty beer bottle on the pavement. Nathan walked up the driveway and skirted the side of the house till he reached the back garden. He wasn't sure what he was looking for. All he knew for certain was that he needed to be here, to find something concrete that would help him come to a conclusion.

He found several plastic garden chairs, two lying on their side, a burned-out braai surrounded by cigarette butts, and empty beer bottles on every surface – all signs of a party attended by a large group of people.

He was studying the contents of a plastic tumbler when the sliding door squealed open and a dark-haired guy stumbled out wearing nothing but a pair of board shorts. Ricardo.

He lit a cigarette and looked up. 'What are you doing here, weirdo?'

Nathan squared his shoulders and put down the tumbler. 'I want to know what happened to Olivia last night.'

Ricardo grinned and shook his head. 'Is that right? Did she send you here?'

'No. I came by myself.' He was being purposefully confrontational. He needed to be, if dealing with an alpha male like Ricardo.

Ricardo flicked his cigarette onto the grass, as if showing Nathan he didn't care. 'Look, retard, nothing happened to Olivia, alright? And nothing she says is going to change that, you understand? No one will believe her anyway.'

'If nothing happened, then why are her clothes ripped?'

Ricardo looked toward the house then stepped forward slowly. 'What did she say to you?' he asked softly.

Nathan stepped back. 'You did something to her, didn't you?'

'Hey, shut up. Everyone was drinking and we were just having a little fun. Me, Olivia, my friends. Don't come here accusing me of ripping girls' clothes.'

'If you didn't do it, then who did? One of your friends?'

'Did what? Nothing happened. Are you deaf as well as retarded?'

'That's not true. You're lying.'

'Says who? You? Olivia?' Ricardo advanced, causing Nathan to take another step back.

A woman's face appeared in the doorway and Ricardo stopped to look back. His angry, pinched face morphed into an innocent expression.

'I thought you said your friends were all gone.'

'They are, Mom. Nathan's here for something else.'

'Well, tell your little friend that unless he wants to help you clean up that mess, he has to go home.'

'Yes, Mom.'

She looked at Nathan curiously before going back inside.

Ricardo turned towards him and glared. 'My parents just got back from a trip. I'm already in trouble for having a party while they were away. I won't let you make it worse with your stupid story. Now get out of here before I throw you out.'

'Then I'm going to the police. If you won't talk to me, you can talk to them.'

Heart in his throat, Nathan turned and hurried back the way he'd come. He didn't know why he'd voiced that empty threat. It was stupid and transparent. But he'd needed to do something to prove he wasn't afraid of Ricardo, even though the guy was older than him and better built.

He reached the middle of the street when running feet made him turn around. Ricardo was hurrying after him.

Nathan stopped and waited, wondering if his threat had worked and if Ricardo was going to try and bargain with him. He didn't expect the fist that came out of nowhere.

'Don't you ever come to my house again! And if you go to the police, I'll break both your legs. Do you understand me, freakshow?'

Lying on the pavement, Nathan tried to cover his head with his arms, but the blows kept coming. He looked helplessly at his own blood splashing onto the cement. He couldn't fight back. Ricardo wasn't giving him a chance to.

'Hold still, Nathan.'

'You're hurting me.'

His mom gripped him under the chin, forcing his head to stay in one position so that she could dab at the raw parts with cotton wool soaked in antiseptic liquid. 'This all started when you brought that girl home. We've never had any trouble with you before.'

'Mom. Stop it.'

'Your mother's right, Nathan. This has got to stop,' said his dad. Out the corner of his eye Nathan could make out his father standing against the kitchen counter with his arms crossed.

'You wanted a normal kid. Isn't this what normal kids do? Go to parties and get into fights. Don't put this on Olivia. She didn't do anything wrong.'

The ball of cotton wool dropped to the floor and his mother looked up in alarm. 'Nathan. We love you. And you are normal. You're just gifted, that's all. What put that silly idea in your head?'

It was too painful to roll his eyes. Had she really forgotten that conversation with her friends? It seemed unlikely, but he'd learned the hard way that his parents had a selective memory, especially where he was concerned. 'Don't worry, Mom,' he said, wincing. He wasn't looking for a fight.

She sucked in her bottom lip, which Nathan knew was her way of stopping herself from crying. She turned away under the pretext of getting more cotton wool.

'So who did this to you? Was it a bully? I'm going to be laying charges against whoever it was,' said his dad.

Nathan remembered his threat. Ricardo wouldn't be able to break his legs from jail, but his friends would. 'I don't want to lay charges. It was my fault anyway. I went looking for a fight.'

His mother threw her arms up in the air. 'This is ridiculous. You're not a boy who goes looking for fights. What's got into you lately?'

The answer hung in the air like an unwelcome guest.

'I have to go check on Olivia,' said Nathan, hopping down from the bar stool.

'She left about an hour ago,' said his dad. 'I saw her sneaking out while I was cutting the grass.'

'*Oh.*'

Nathan caught a glimpse of his reflection in the hall mirror. His face was as swollen as it felt. He also saw the unhappy expressions on his parents' faces, as well as their disappointment.

His mother sniffed loudly and closed the first-aid box. 'I need your shirt so I can wash the blood out of it. Your jeans too.'

'Okay. I'll go change.'

He left his parents in the kitchen, all the time wondering about Olivia. He needed to check if she was okay. He was too concerned about her pain to worry about his.

30

The school morning passed for Nathan in a half-aware fog. At break, he sat on the step and tried to eat his sandwich through swollen lips. Patches of bright-green leaves were sprouting out the bare, spindly branches. The grass had swelled up after months of rain.

He opened his lunchbox and took out the other half of his sandwich to examine. It was leftover roast beef and beetroot, which had stained the bread pink. He took a bite, his teeth crushing a piece of cold onion. It wasn't bad. As a kid he and his dad used to eat the leftovers of roasts on bread as a special treat. It tasted like a happy memory.

He hadn't seen Olivia yet, as their next class together was only after lunch. He wondered if she'd even come to school. He'd tried to message her, but she hadn't replied. He really hoped she was okay. If she wasn't in the next class, he'd go to her house after school to check on her. In fact, he decided, he might not even stay the whole day, and bunk the last class.

Nathan popped the last piece of his sandwich in his mouth

and pushed it to the left side where it hurt less. When he looked up, she was standing in front of him, looking at the ground with the same lifeless expression.

He jumped up, sending his lunchbox clattering to the ground. 'Olivia! Hi. Do you want to sit down?'

She took a seat on the step without a word and slouched her shoulders. Looking sideways, she studied his face and frowned. 'I'm sorry you got beaten up. Everyone's talking about it.'

'Don't worry about me. How are you doing? You didn't reply to my messages last night.'

She sighed. 'I didn't want to talk.'

'Okay.' He hovered uncertainly in front of her, and looked from side to side to make sure no-one was within listening distance. 'Are you sure you want to be here today? I saw Ricardo earlier.'

She sighed again. 'It doesn't matter, Nate. I don't care.'

He cringed. 'Don't call me that. I don't like it.'

'Fine. Nathan. Whatever. Is it okay if I stay here for break? I know you probably hate me.'

'I don't.'

Her face was all scrunched up and her bottom lip trembled like she was about to cry. 'You know I didn't even like him. I was just trying to make Virginie jealous. I thought if it looked like I was dating someone older and popular, it would eat her alive.'

'We don't have to talk about it ...'

She wiped her nose. 'And the rumour about you and me, I didn't want people to know because they'd just ruin it, not because I'm embarrassed about you.'

Oh.

'But it all backfired, didn't it?' she said bitterly.

'I hate it when you're sad.'

She bowed her head and bit down on her lip. When she looked up, her eyes were glossy-wet with tears. She wiped them away hurriedly with her sleeve. 'I'm not sad. I told you, I don't feel anything.'

'You have to feel something. We can't just leave it. We have to tell someone.'

'No.' Her expression was fierce.

'But why?'

'Because nothing happened, Nathan. I don't want to talk about it.'

'But you have to. I haven't seen you smile in forever.'

She looked away. 'What's there to smile about?'

'Otters. They make you smile.'

Her expression tightened, and then she was smiling and laughing and crying at the same time, which he thought was completely unfair because it made reading her face impossible.

'Why are you looking at me like that?' she said.

'I'm waiting for you to stop laughing so I can work out what you're thinking because you're not telling me anything.'

'I'm not thinking about anything, alright?' She wiped her eyes with her sleeve again. 'I really am sorry about everything. You don't have to believe me if you don't want to. I was really awful to you.'

'Don't worry about it.'

'Ricardo and I were never really together. Not like that, anyway. Not like it was with you. I wanted everyone to think we were. I should've just listened to you.'

'I need you to be honest with me, Olivia. I need to know what happened on Saturday night. You're telling me and not telling me at the same time. You came to me, so why can't you just be straight with me?'

She sniffed loudly and looked away. 'Are you ever going to leave it alone? I was drunk, okay? Everyone was. It all got out of hand. I really don't want to talk about it.'

'What happened?'

She shrugged, and tugged at her shoelace. 'Seriously, Nathan, it was my fault. I led them on. Can we drop it now?'

'Them?'

'Ricardo and his friends,' she said, sniffing.

He inhaled sharply. 'You have to tell someone.'

'No. It's bad enough that you know. And now Ricardo knows you know. You can't tell anyone else.'

'Why?'

'Because I say so,' she snapped.

'Did he threaten you? He threatened me.'

'He didn't threaten me. I just want to forget about it, okay?'

Birds twittered in the silence. Nathan sat down on the cement and stared at his feet. 'This isn't fair,' he said.

'Life isn't fair. Get over it.'

Nathan was beginning to dread the English classroom with its old-fashioned posters of Shakespearean plays featuring ancient actors who were probably all dead. The first thing he noticed when he entered was Mandy and her friends chuckling over a cellphone. It didn't take superior observational skills to realise what they found amusing: they looked up at Olivia walking in behind him and immediately descended into a giggling huddle.

Another rumour.

He waited for Olivia to sit down before doing the same.

211

Miss Tomlinson noticed his face and frowned to herself, shaking her head, as she distributed worksheets. He wondered if she thought he'd beaten himself up, because that's how she was acting – like it was his fault.

'I find the best way to prepare for exams is to know your subject matter. So today we'll be doing character sketches. Put your hand up if you get stuck and I'll come help you.'

Nathan took out his setwork book and slapped it on his desk, then picked up the worksheet. *List ten features about the appearance of the character Desdemona.*

He turned to Olivia, but she hadn't looked at the worksheet yet. She was staring at her phone. He caught the frightened look she was trying to conceal. 'What's up?' he whispered.

She looked up blankly and smiled. It was totally fake. 'Nothing.'

'Let me see.'

Before she could resist, he grabbed the phone out of her hand. On the screen was a picture of Olivia with one of the grade 11 guys on top of her. The rest of them were standing in the background. *It's a fake. It must be a fake.* But he could see that no-one had done this in Photoshop. He minimised the picture and saw she had been tagged in the picture on Instagram.

He killed the screen and slipped the phone into his pocket. He felt disconnected. Unplugged. *Don't freak out. Focus on the facts.*

He looked to the front of the class. Mandy had her phone out and was waving it in their direction.

He turned to Olivia. Her cheeks were red, but she was staring resolutely forward, pretending that nothing was wrong. She was wearing that same faraway expression that had frightened him to death the day before.

Nathan bit down hard on his tongue. They were all in on it. Mandy, Ricardo, all of them. They all knew about what had happened. To them, it was funny, something to laugh about. They were all protecting each other against Olivia. Against him. They wanted Olivia to know that they knew and that they didn't care.

He didn't understand. He felt like he was falling.

He was still staring at her when she looked up, meeting his gaze.

'I'm fine,' she mouthed.

'I'm not.'

Under the table she took his hand. 'Try to be,' she whispered.

31

How could they talk about something so monumentally horrible?

Nathan stared at Olivia helplessly, while she stared at nothing. He couldn't even play music on his phone because the thought of music seemed disrespectful in the situation. What was even more worrying was the fact that she wasn't even crying. She just stared into space, like she'd done on Saturday morning.

So many things were going on in his head. He couldn't talk to anyone about it, least of all his parents. How could he? They would just freak out and want to go to the police, and Olivia was dead against that. He didn't know what she was thinking. She was acting weird and it terrified him.

He'd learned not to trust people, but never for one second did he think that his classmates were actually capable of pure evil.

'Are you going to be okay?'

'I'm fine.'

'You keep saying that, but I'm not sure if I believe you.'

She looked at him with dull, expressionless eyes. 'Please go home. I'll be fine.'

'You're being way too calm about this.'

'Stop worrying about my state of mind.' She smiled and edged to the side of her bed. 'I'll be back. I just need to use the bathroom.'

When she was gone he punched the mattress. It had started out so innocently. All she'd wanted was to be part of a group of friends. He'd thought he could help her. It had never occurred to him that it would get so out of hand, that it would lead to a monstrous cyberbullying campaign.

The white bedroom walls were still dotted with Prestik and bits of paper that had survived her purge. He got up and began scratching them all away, thinking that if he got rid of all the traces, it wouldn't remind her of any of those people. He felt useless. Worse than useless. He felt like a failure.

When he was finished with the wall, he went to empty the wastepaper basket, which also still contained all the torn-up pictures. He passed Olivia's grandmother in the lounge watching soap operas. She didn't greet him, so he didn't greet her either.

Olivia hadn't told her mother about what had happened, and he wasn't sure she ever would. He couldn't accept that she didn't want to tell anyone, and didn't want to do anything about it, rather pretending that nothing had happened. But who was he to judge? He was doing exactly the same thing. They were both cowards.

He returned to her room. Olivia wasn't back from the bathroom yet. Nathan peeked out the door and down the passage. The bathroom door was wide open, and the room was empty.

He stepped out into the passage. 'Olivia?'

He'd just been in the kitchen and he knew she wasn't in the lounge. A gentle breeze tickled his neck. He turned around and saw a door open at the end of the passage leading to the back garden.

He ran.

He found her sitting against the wall at the end of the garden, folded up into the smallest size she could make herself. She looked up as he approached, her face streaked with tears. He slowed down, feeling lost and inside out, and started wringing his hands. 'I knew you weren't fine,' he said.

She said nothing.

'Come back inside, please.'

When she didn't answer, he walked forward, but before he could reach her, she lifted up her arm and opened her hand. It was caked in bright red blood. In the centre of her palm was a slim razor blade.

He froze. 'What did you do?'

Had he shouted? He wasn't sure. His ears were ringing.

'It was my dad's. I found it in the bathroom. I think ... I think this is the right decision. Then everyone will be happy.'

He slipped on the grass in his haste to get to her. He shook as he lifted up her right wrist where she'd slashed herself. Blood streaked her arm and dripped from her elbow into the grass below.

'I cut upwards, like you're supposed to.'

He grabbed her around her waist and tried to pull her up, but she was being stubborn.

'Get up, Olivia. Please.'

She'd gone quiet again. The sky exploded in his head, blinding him, deafening him, searing his skin.

'Olivia... please ... Olivia, come on ... Somebody, help me! Help!'

32

'I need a lift to the hospital.'

Nathan's parents shared a look. His mother picked up the remote to turn off the television and the *MasterChef* contestants blipped out of existence.

His dad coughed into his fist to clear his throat. 'We don't think that's a good idea, kiddo.'

'Why not?'

His father motioned towards the couch. 'Can you sit down, maybe? It's difficult to talk to you standing in the doorway.'

Nathan stomped into the room and fell onto a sofa. He hadn't slept. His eyes were burning. 'I'm waiting,' he said.

His dad leaned forward and steepled his hands. 'This has been difficult for all of us. And we've tried to be as supportive as we can, but enough is enough. You were beaten up. We still don't know by who. You won't tell us anything. And then you come home covered in blood because your girlfriend tried to kill herself.'

'She's not my girlfriend.'

'That's not the point, Nathan. The point is we're worried about you and we've given you enough freedom up to now. It's time to rein back. For everyone's sake.'

'You can't stop me from seeing Olivia. I'll see her at school anyway, when she gets released from hospital. You're just delaying the inevitable.'

His parents exchanged another glance and his father cleared his throat. 'Please hear us out before you react. We were thinking that it might be in everyone's best interest if we looked at other schools that are better suited to your talents.'

'You want me to change schools? Are you serious?' Nathan's heart began to pound. He didn't need this. Not now.

'You've been having more and more panic attacks recently and we'd feel a lot better if you were in a school more prepared to handle that.'

'That's not true. You just don't want me to see Olivia, and you're using my ASD against me. That's not fair!' He scrambled to his feet. 'You don't care about me at all!'

'Nathan, we wouldn't be having this conversation if we didn't care about you.'

'I'll just walk to the hospital. You can't stop me from going outside.'

'Nathan, stop shouting and sit down.'

The sound of his father's raised voice made him obey. He hated himself for it.

'Listen to me. I'm asking you nicely now. We need you to distance yourself from that girl for a while. Can you do that? For me?'

'I told her I was going to visit her every night.'

'Well, you're not going to tonight.'

Nathan shook his head. 'You act like you get it, and then you turn around and say something different. You're a hypocrite.'

Nathan's mom raised her hands to her mouth. 'Nathan.'

'It's okay, he's just angry. Everyone just calm down.'

'You don't have to explain my own mood to me like I'm not even in the room!'

Nathan stood up and went to his room, slamming the door behind him. A couple of his Lego mini-figures tumbled off the shelf.

He was shaking again. He'd been shaking for weeks. They didn't understand the seriousness of the situation. He paced his room, muttering to himself. *One hundred. Ninety-nine. Ninety-eight.*

He sat down on the bed and breathed into his cupped hands. There was nothing he could do. He couldn't be emotional. He had to collect his thoughts. Focus.

He pulled his phone out of his pocket. *I can't come tonight. Dad's being impossible.* He watched the screen till he got a response.

Okay.

How are you?

Alive. I even suck at killing myself.

Don't say that.

You'll come tomorrow, right?

Of course.

He wished those jerks from school knew what they'd done. He wished they felt what he felt, that white-hot pain that never went away. If only they could feel just a fraction of what Olivia was feeling. He didn't understand how they could feel nothing. No guilt. No remorse.

When Olivia didn't reply he sent her another message. *What did the doctor say?*

That I'm stupid.

What did he really say?

He called me stupid. He said it was a very stupid thing I did. Like I'm a child.

That wasn't cool. Did he see your bruises? Did you tell the social worker?

Why would anyone care?

I care.

Do you know why I like you, Nathan?

Why?

Because you think differently to other people. You see the world so clearly. You see people for what they really are. You see me.

This wasn't how the world was supposed to work. Police arrested the bad guys. Criminals showed remorse. Hospitals cared about their patients. Didn't anyone care any more?

He cared. He cared more than anything. He had to do something to show them. No one else was going to do anything. It was up to him. He had to prove it to himself. He had to prove it to Olivia.

33

Nathan clutched the straps of his backpack tightly as he stalked down the hallway.

The cut on his mouth was a black bruise that made his bottom lip protrude. He had a matching bruise under his right eye.

The grade 11 guys sniggered when he passed them. *Let them*, he thought. They didn't even register on his radar. He didn't even try to stop muttering. He needed to focus.

He would have to wait till lunch break to execute his plan, but that gave him lots of time to prepare himself. It was a risky move that made his chest tight, but it was worth it. The idea swam around in his head, making him dizzy and feverish. He was manic, and that was perfect. It put him in the zone. It would stop him from failing. When he really put his mind to something, he could do anything.

He stared fixedly at his watch, counting down till break time.

It was a relief knowing that the news about Olivia's attempted suicide hadn't leaked at school. As far as anyone was concerned, she was just absent. He was sure Virginie and the rest of them were pleased. Their disgusting stunt with the picture was the talk of the school. He wished he could erase it from every phone in the building.

Don't think about that.

Nathan nodded to himself and rocked back and forth in his gaming chair. Getting payback was the only thing getting him through class. The giggles, the rumours, none of it mattered. He had a mission.

At break time he settled underneath his tree and cracked his knuckles. He pulled his lunchbox out of his bag and opened it. There were no sandwiches inside, just electronics.

Nathan bent down and set to work. He picked up the modified cellphone and started connecting wires. It was one of his dad's old phones that he didn't use any more since he'd got his upgrade. Nathan had found it at the back of the kitchen drawer into which his parents usually threw broken appliances and old batteries in case Nathan felt the urge to tinker. His dad wouldn't even notice the phone was missing.

Nathan had spent the entire night working on his wireless signal jammer. He hadn't had to use an online tutorial: the blueprints were all in his mind.

He planned to target the large electronic billboard that the school used to rent out advertising space for extra income. It was situated at the far corner of the sports field where everyone spent break, but it was so large that it was visible from every angle and could be seen by everyone outside.

It was perfect.

Nathan smiled to himself. The only protection was a CCTV camera, as if the principal expected someone to go up and vandalise the billboard manually. Idiot. Anything that worked on a wireless network could be hacked. He was doing the school a service, really. He was showing them a fundamental fault in their security system.

Nathan eased the last wire into place. It struck him that he would be seen as the obvious culprit, but he didn't care. Someone had to do something, and since Olivia wouldn't let him go to the police, he would just have to let people know some other way.

His way.

He turned the jammer on and waved it around till he found the signal. Above him, the billboard screen flickered and the giant picture of the toothy grin broke up into nothingness. Nathan uploaded his own code. It was that easy.

It didn't occur to him that it wouldn't work. He knew it would. Everything he built worked.

The second step was getting rid of the evidence. He used the lid of his lunchbox to dig a hole at the base of the tree. Then, carefully wrapping the cellphone in plastic, he buried it.

He stood up to admire his handiwork.

Nothing happened at first, but then one or two people noticed and started pointing. The message spread like a virus. More people turned around, then more, until everyone was facing the billboard. Even people inside the school had come outside to look.

The field had gone quiet. No one was laughing now.

He looked over to the group of girls sitting a few metres away. Virginie's mouth was open. Her eyes wide. She was horrified.

Good.

Nathan's way was more effective and much quicker than any

rumour. His message couldn't be misunderstood. It was written in simple English, in black and white, for everyone to see.

Ricardo Ferreira is a rapist.

Virginie Rands is a racist and a bully.

They are both criminals.

Cyberbullying is a crime. Rape is a crime.

#LockThemUp

But that wasn't all. As he stood admiring his handiwork, everyone started reaching for their phones. He'd sent malware to the computer that managed the school email lists and WhatsApp groups. As soon as the secretary opened the anonymous email he'd sent, his special message would be sent out across all channels, multiple times. Hundreds of times. Thousands of times. The poor school system administrator would have no way of stopping it until the message had been sent out to every phone number and email address in the school database.

Next, his virus would infect and spread across the school servers. Every computer and device connected to the school server would display the same message. And it couldn't be deleted.

34

Nathan told Olivia everything. She even listened to the complicated parts about how he'd hijacked the wireless signal. The story had made the news, and pictures of Virginie and Ricardo were all over the internet.

'Everyone is posting their own bad experiences with Virginie and Ricardo on Instagram. The school has expelled them both,' he said.

He'd been worried about her reaction, but that haunted look was gone. She looked at him in wonder, her white hospital blanket clutched in her fingers beneath her chin. 'I'm surprised they didn't expel you too. I mean, it was obviously you behind it. No one else has skills like yours.'

'They had no proof. I buried the signal jammer, remember? And I'm invisible to most people, anyway.'

Olivia half-smiled, filling his insides with delicious warmth. It had been worth it, just for that.

'How long was the billboard up for?'

'The whole day. Mr Willis didn't know how to turn it off.

They ended up ripping the wiring out and short-circuiting the entire thing.'

'Wow.'

'The computers all had to be turned off too.'

Nathan was jittery with pride. He reached across the bed and touched Olivia's hand, then quickly drew back. He'd wanted to hold her hand but her wrist was wrapped in bandages and didn't want to transfer germs to the wound.

'How long do you have to stay here for?' he asked.

'I'm under psychiatric watch so I'm here for at least a week. Then I have to go to a stepdown clinic. They give me pills once a day and I don't even know what they are.'

He reckoned it was some kind of antidepressant, but he didn't voice this thought. 'You look better,' he said, instead.

'Maybe they're happy pills, then.'

'I wish there was more I could do. What happened to you … it wasn't cool. They shouldn't just get away with it.'

'I don't know if I can face what comes after laying criminal charges. Going to court, the physical examination. The police came to see me already and I gave a statement, but it's up to me whether I press charges or not. I turned sixteen in January, so legally they can't make me.'

'Are you going to?'

'I don't know.' She turned her face the window. 'It's humiliating. And I was drunk. That's all anyone is going to care about.'

'No one cares about that.'

'Yes, they do. In court, they're going to bring it up. What was I wearing, how much I'd been drinking, going over every second of that night over and over again.'

He dropped his head into his hands, all happiness gone.

'This is so unfair. I thought that if I revealed the truth, then justice would play out.'

She reached across and lightly touched his fingers. 'Hey, it's okay. At least I have you back. I almost pushed you away.'

'You did push me away. Several times.'

She frowned. 'Being around nasty people makes you nasty. Maybe if I hang around you more, some of that genius will rub off on me.'

'You can't catch genius,' he said, pressing his fingertips against hers.

His phone vibrated on the bedside table and he sighed. 'That's my fifteen minutes up,' he said.

'I can't believe your dad put you under house arrest for something that wasn't even officially your doing.'

'He doesn't need evidence. He's my dad. He knows it was me. But he let me see you. That's something.'

He waited for her to smile again before leaving, but it didn't come.

'I'll see you soon,' he said.

35

'Come on, Nathan. We can go into the iStore on the way out. I'm in a hurry.'

Nathan grudgingly peeled himself away from the window display. 'I'm not five years old, Mom. I don't need you to accompany me into a shop.'

'Yes, but you're still grounded. Now, come on.'

His hands in his pockets and his eyes rolling into the back of his eyelids, Nathan followed his mother down the glimmering passage. It was only October, but the mall had already put out all its Christmas decorations. A giant glittery ornament dangled dangerously above his head, its point trained down on his skull. He skirted out the way of its trajectory.

His mother had insisted he go with her to the mall because he needed new shirts. They'd headed towards the clothing stores, but then, curiously, his mother had walked past them. His suspicion had deepened when she'd made straight for the escalator, heading towards the food court. She was up to something.

He followed her into Panarottis pizzeria and his eyes widened when he saw who was waiting for them inside: Mohendra and his mother. She was dressed all in purple like a giant beetroot.

'What's going on? What are they doing here?' he asked.

'I called them and told them to meet us here,' she said.

'Why?'

'Because I'm tired of you moping around the house all day.'

She looked away quickly, an indication that she wasn't being altogether truthful. He suspected she wanted to bring Mohendra back into his life so he didn't see Olivia as often.

Mrs Chetty squeezed herself out of the vinyl booth and nodded in greeting. 'Hello, Nathan. Good to see you.'

'Hello.' He didn't believe a word of it.

She motioned for him to take her seat, which he did reluctantly. It was warm and he was forced to face Mohendra, who was staring intently at his milkshake. His mother and Mrs Chetty started walking away.

'Wait, where are you going?' Nathan called.

'I'm taking Indira for coffee. Have fun,' his mother replied over her shoulder.

Indira? Since when were they on a first-name basis?

The mothers left, and the two ex-best-friends found themselves alone.

Nathan sat up uncomfortably in the booth and looked everywhere but at Mohendra, who did the same. There was nothing to look at other than the other customers and the old-fashioned décor. This went on for some time, when the arrival of a large vegetarian pizza forced them both to look up at the same time.

Mohendra quickly shifted his focus to a slice of pizza. 'Your mom could've at least picked a better restaurant.'

Nathan had gone through too much recently, reducing his

patience to zero. 'Do you even remember why we're fighting?' he asked.

Mohendra looked up. 'Because you insulted my mother.'

'Really? That's why you haven't been speaking to me for a month? Because you misheard me.'

Mohendra blushed and chewed determinedly on a mouthful of pizza and swallowed. 'You did insult my mother.'

'I didn't. I called you selfish.' Nathan scooped up a slice of pizza and aggressively bit off a corner. 'And anyway, you were the one who overreacted and deleted me everywhere. That wasn't cool.'

Mohendra bent his head and loudly sucked up the remainder of his milkshake. They went back to avoiding each other's gaze.

When Mohendra pushed his empty glass away, a waiter in a light green uniform magically appeared. 'Can I get you another one?'

Mohendra jerked back in fright. 'Ja, sure, whatever.'

'And for you?' the waiter asked Nathan with a broad, insincere smile.

'Uh, a Coke please.'

'Got it.'

'What a weirdo,' sniggered Mohendra once the waiter had left.

Nathan grinned. He hadn't realised how much he'd missed his best friend making fun of random people. Mohendra was a self-confessed drama queen and Nathan liked that about him.

The boys looked at each other, then stared off in separate directions. Their drinks arrived, and Nathan waited for the witty remark, but Mohendra didn't comment. They continued eating in silence.

'Where did you get that shiner from?' asked Mohendra after a while.

Nathan chewed on the inside of his cheek. 'A chop at school.'

'Nice. It makes you look hardcore.'

'Okay. If you say so.'

Mohendra was staring at him. 'Are you still helping that Olivia girl?'

Nathan sank back in his seat. 'I don't want to talk about that.'

Mohendra shook his head. 'Girls. I did warn you.'

'You were right. Mostly. But not about Olivia.'

'Okay, okay. She's a no-go zone. I get it.'

Nathan remembered where they'd left off the last time they spoke. 'Did you ever hook up with Karen?'

Mohendra bolted upright. 'What d'you think I've been doing these past few weeks? Turns out she was totally into me.' He slumped back down and added. 'We broke up last week. I'm pretty heartbroken.'

'I'm sorry.'

'It's fine. Karma's a bitch.'

Nathan listened while Mohendra's voice filled the silence. They had a lot to catch up on. Nathan preferred to listen. He didn't want to talk about Olivia, so he heard Mohendra's tale of heartbreak, and also the repercussions of the night he came home drunk. It had taken him a while to convince his mother that he wouldn't go out drinking again, and even longer to convince her that it hadn't been Nathan's fault. Nathan listened to how his best friend had defended him to his mother, and yet he'd refused to communicate with him. He suspected that pride had had a part to play. Human beings were strange, strange creatures.

They finished their drinks and wandered off in the direction of the arcade. Mohendra bought tokens, which he stuffed into his hoodie pockets.

'Aw, man, they still have the old Street Fighter games here. And Mortal Kombat. Joh, when was the last time you played that?'

'Years ago.'

'Let's do it.'

They spent a small fortune trying to beat the top score on the pixelated screen.

'This is going to give me epilepsy or something,' said Mohendra after their sixth game.

Nathan thought the game was clumsy and slow, but he would never admit that. He was extremely grateful to his mother for what she'd done, even if she'd done it for the wrong reasons. He'd thought he was never going to see Mohendra again, and now it felt like they were right back to where they'd been before the fight.

Life wasn't necessarily back to normal, but he would take what he could get.

Nathan held up a lifelike otter plush toy he had found at Toys R Us.

Olivia squealed in delight.

'I'm going to name him George. Or Barnaby. He looks like a Barnaby.'

He liked that she was happy with his gift. Her smile made everything better. He sat up straighter in the hard visitor's chair. 'I saw my friend Mohendra today.'

'Is he that friend you said goes to another school?' she asked.

He grinned. She remembered. 'Ja. We had a fight, but we made up.'

'That's good. I guess now you won't have to come babysit me all the time.'

She turned away, and it took every bit of willpower not to reach across and pull her face back towards him.

'I'll always visit you. I want to. You know that.'

She swung her head back towards him. 'You mean it?'

'Of course.'

Olivia beamed at her new pet and swung it back and forth in a swimming motion.

Nathan had searched the entire mall for something beautiful, something vibrant. He was pleased with his decision.

'Mandy's gone.'

He'd been waiting to tell her, but he didn't know how.

Her eyes popped open in shock. 'What?'

'Her parents took her out of school shortly after Virginie was expelled. People weren't standing for her bullying any more.'

'Ha. That's brilliant. You really are amazing,' she said.

He shrugged. 'I didn't do anything really. Just some dumb hacking.'

'You're always there to help me. Even when I'm horrible to you.'

'I'm horrible to you sometimes too. You told me that.'

'I didn't mean it like that. You can't help it.' She eased herself back down and looked at him. 'Tell me about the robot. Did you finish it?'

'Yes. It's not a big deal. It does what it's supposed to.'

She smiled. 'Tell me anyway.'

So he did. She closed her eyes a few sentences in, but he carried on, even though he knew she wasn't going to understand any of it. He told her about his Minecraft server too, and the new game about Pirates he and Mohendra had started playing.

His dad hadn't messaged him to say his time with her was up, so he stayed till a nurse chased him out. He hoped that meant his punishment was over.

EPILOGUE

They arrived early on a bright morning, the leftover shadows of night still receding.

Olivia struggled under the weight of a picnic basket.

'I can take that for you,' he said.

'No, I'm fine. You're carrying too much already.'

That wasn't strictly true. He had a rolled-up blanket and a backpack containing her sketch pad and pencils and his comic books. He could easily have carried the basket as well but she was determined to prove that she was okay.

They trekked up and down Kirstenbosch Garden, looking for the right spot. Some of the nicer areas, like the grassy slope near Van Riebeeck's Hedge, were roped off for the summer concerts. Another favourite of hers was a grassy patch near the bronze otter statue, but it was occupied by a family. So they continued to search.

The air smelled of summer and pungent herbs, like lavender and buchu, and fynbos. From the path he watched as she dashed across a flowerbed he was sure they weren't supposed to walk on.

'Come on,' she called.

Her hair was loose and flying in all directions, and her sandals were already off and stuffed into the back pockets of her shorts. He hesitated before following, doing his best not to tramp on any of the plants.

Still leaning sideways under the weight of the basket, Olivia headed towards the river covered in lily pads. He caught up quickly.

'There's a bench over there,' she said, attempting to blow hair out of her face.

He leaned across and took the basket from her.

'Thanks,' she said.

He dumped the picnic basket unceremoniously on the grass and ran to the riverbank to join her.

'There're freshwater crabs between the rocks. We might be lucky today.'

He looked to where she was pointing, but even if he narrowed his eyes, he couldn't see any crabs. He could see rocks, and moss and even tadpoles, but no crabs.

'Where?'

'There,' she said, pointing. 'You're just cursed to never see anything,' she said, shaking her head and smiling.

'I guess so.'

He went back to the bench and laid the blanket out on the grass. His mother had bought mini cheese puffs and some crisps for him to take along, and Olivia had made cheese muffins. All the bottoms were burnt.

'Mmm, carbs,' she said, turning around to see what he was doing.

'I'm sorry, I didn't know you were on a diet. I just told my mom to buy everything you might like.'

'I'm not on a diet. And you're very sweet.'

He was relieved that she wasn't watching her food intake. She was thinner from her stay in hospital.

He stuffed a handful of crisps into his mouth and continued to pack out the rest of the food.

Mohendra had told him not to overthink the things she said but rather to just accept them. It had saved him a lot of effort. Not overanalysing every little thing she did or said meant more time to enjoy her company.

His father had given him similar advice. *Never try to understand women, Nathan. Trust me. Just don't.* Nathan was still dubious about his father's advice. After all, he kept changing his mind about Olivia. One day she was a bad influence, the next she wasn't. It was confusing.

A splash made him look up. She was negotiating her way through the river, wading unsteadily towards a tree trunk that had been blown over on to its side. She was looking for otters, and that meant she was happy. She'd almost given up on them because of all the teasing at school. He was happy she hadn't. He was worried that the guys who'd attacked her had taken some of her joy away. It was a relief to know that she was able to shine.

He smoothed out a corner of the blanket that had been blown over by the wind and anchored the paper napkins with a tub of cream cheese.

He hadn't been surprised when she invited him for a picnic.

She was really trying to prove that she wanted him around. They'd been messaging each other every night. It really felt like he had the old Olivia back. So far, she hadn't done anything to make him doubt his own sanity. Still, he needed to tread carefully.

He watched her make her wobbly way back, one foot in front of the other to stop herself from falling, her ankles splashed with mud.

Her face opened up into a grin when she saw him watching her. 'They're hiding from me,' she said.

'Not a bad idea. I would hide from you.'

She ran towards him and pushed him onto his back, then sank to her knees and kissed him. He looked at her in surprise. So they were back to that level of intimacy.

His fingers trembled as he reached out to put his arms around her, and their kiss deepened. This is what he wanted and that frightened him. Was she ready? Was he? Was this brief moment of happiness worth the pain that was sure to come?

He pulled away. 'We don't have to do this. I'm happy to just be around you. I'm not expecting more than that. I don't want you to feel—'

'Nathan, stop. You're thinking too much. Just chill.'

'Yes, sir!'

She laughed and kissed him lightly on the nose. 'You're ridiculous sometimes, but in a good way.'

Despite his fears that this joy wouldn't last, it was an amazing day. He read his *Ultimate Avengers* graphic novel while she sketched the ferns that curled above the water's surface. She drew really well. More than once he stopped reading to watch her.

Later, she picked at a muffin while she gazed at the water. She hadn't touched the cheese puffs.

'Please eat something,' he said.

'I'm not hungry.'

'Try.'

She leaned across and bit the end off a cheese puff he was holding. 'Happy?'

'Yes.'

'Stop waiting for me to break, Nathan. I'm okay. Treat me like you would at any other time.'

He reached across and pulled the hair out of her face. Her eyes were bright again.

'I'm the one who might break,' he said. 'Everything feels ... I don't know how to explain. Everything feels so fragile. I don't want to lose this.'

'You won't. I'm not going anywhere. Not this time.'

He nodded. Losing her had become his greatest fear. It closed his chest and haunted him at night. He gripped her fingers tightly, afraid that if he let go, terrible things would happen.

They went for a walk. This time he insisted on carrying everything. They didn't spot any otters, although he looked very hard for one to prove to himself that they existed.

They dropped their gear under a Cape holly tree and sank down to the grass, eyes closed. It didn't matter that there were lots of people in the gardens – there always were when the weather was good. They were invisible, for all he cared. He just wanted to kiss her. He never wanted to stop kissing her.

'I like that you've never kissed anyone before. It's like you're mine, all mine. Untainted by the world,' she said.

He studied their interlaced fingers. Hers were so much smaller than his. 'Do you mean that?'

'I said so, didn't I?'

He smiled. He liked that she remembered the things he'd said. He'd always thought he was the only person who remembered everything. She kept surprising him.

He hoped she never stopped.

Printed in the United States
by Baker & Taylor Publisher Services